AESOP'S
FABLES

AESOP'S FABLES

The Cruelty of the Gods

CARLO GÉBLER

Illustrations by

GAVIN WESTON

Interlink Books

An imprint of Interlink Publishing Group, Inc.
Northampton, Massachusetts

First American edition published in 2020 by

Interlink Books
An imprint of Interlink Publishing Group, Inc.
46 Crosby Street, Northampton, MA 01060
www.interlinkbooks.com

Library of Congress Cataloging-in-Publication data available:
ISBN-13: 978-1-62371-950-0

Printed and bound in the United States of America

Carlo Gébler:

For Sam, Bill and Noah

Gavin Weston:

For Holly and Adam

This book belongs to ...

....

CONTENTS

1: CAPRICE, ARROGANCE AND THE EXERCISE OF ARBITRARY POWER

2: Irreconcilability, Conflict and Vengeance

3: Self-Deception, Stupidity and Idiocy

4: Ambition, Overweening and Overreach

5: Selfishness, Self-Interest and Self-Love

6: Gloating and Heartlessness

7: Jealousy, Covetousness and Greed

8: CUNNING, GUILE AND INSIGHT

9: BITTER WORDS, REBUKES, BARBS AND SAVAGERIES

10: Last Griefs or a Series of Epilogues

'A fable is a bridge that leads to truth.'
Racial Proverbs, S.G. Champion, 1950

ABOUT THE CONTRIBUTORS

Aesop is allegedly the author of a collection of Greek fables. Whether he existed or not is moot, though many attempts were made in ancient times to establish Aesop as a person. Herodotus said he lived in the sixth century BC and was a slave. Plutarch made him an adviser to Croesus, king of Lydia. A first-century Egyptian hagiography has him as a slave on the island of Samos who then went on to serve the King of Babylon, among others. In all probability Aesop was an invention created to dignify fabular materials with an author, and as a result the fable form and the name became synonymous. On the other hand, perhaps there really was an Aesop ...

Carlo Gébler was born in Dublin in 1954 and lives outside Enniskillen, Northern Ireland. He is the author of novels including *The Innocent of Falkland Road*, short story collections including *The Wing Orderly's Tales*, and the memoirs *Father & I* and *The Projectionist: The Story of Ernest Gébler*. He has also written novels for children and plays for radio and the stage, including *10 Rounds*, which was shortlisted for the Christopher Ewart-Biggs Memorial Prize. From 1991 to 1997 he taught in HMP Maze, and from 1997 to 2015 he was writer-in-residence in HMP Maghaberry. He currently teaches at Trinity College Dublin, and the American College, as well as Hydebank Wood College where he works with young male and female prisoners. He is a member of Aosdána.

Gavin Weston was born in Belfast in 1962. He lives on the Ards Peninsula with an ancient dog and a cantankerous parrot. He studied Fine Art at Central Saint Martins and Goldsmiths, London, before moving to Niger where he taught English and worked for the American NGO Africare. Returning to Ireland, he taught art (at Belfast Metropolitan College and Ulster University) while continuing to exhibit and create a number of prize-winning public artworks. He is the author of the novel *Harmattan*, set in West Africa, and was a columnist for *The Sunday Times* for many years. Working as writer-in-residence at HMP Magilligan, he met and became friends with Carlo Gébler and founded and edited the prison magazine *TIME IN*. Gavin is an ambassador and passionate advocate for the London-based NGO, FORWARD, which campaigns to end child marriage.

INTRODUCTION

I

The *Oxford English Dictionary* describes a fable as a story not founded on fact. It doesn't define an Aesop fable but perhaps a workable definition might be: a story not founded on fact that comes with a moral attached. This combination has always been a difficult proposition. When story and moral work in harmony, the reader experiences an 'Oh yes ...' moment and a rush of pleasure, but when story and moral are not in harmony, the reader experiences an 'Oh no ...' moment and a jolt of displeasure. We will always hate what 'has a palpable design upon us', said Keats, speaking of poetry though his argument applies to all literary forms, and certainly, as far as Aesop's work is concerned, many readers, especially modern ones, have spurned it because of morals that are too obvious, too insistent or too bumptious.

II

Whether or not there was an actual Aesop, who wrote the fables that carry his name, is contested. Martin Luther, the theologian, believed Aesop was a fiction. However, should we prefer to believe there was such a figure, then we can turn to the *Life of Aesop*, an ancient Greek text of uncertain provenance. It was probably composed sometime during the first century A.D. and it almost certainly recycles material from earlier accounts of Aesop's life.

Aesop, according to the *Life of Aesop*, is born sometime in the fifth century B.C. (so about five or six hundred years before the composition of the *Life*). His place of birth is variously stated as Thrace, Phrygia, Ethiopia, Samos, Athens or Sardis. Physically he is dark-skinned (it is said his name derives from *Aethiop*, meaning Ethiopian) and he is hobbled by a long list of physical deformities: a swollen head, squint eyes, a fat lip, a snub nose, short arms, a pot belly, a hunched back, flat-feet, bandy legs and (in the language of the day) dwarfish stature. He also has a serious speech impediment or might even be mute.

Aesop is born a slave or captured at an early age and made a slave. At some point (in adolescence or very early adulthood) he treats a priestess of the goddess Isis with such kindness that she gives him the gift of speech. He immediately uses his new talent to denounce his overseer to his master as a vicious, vindictive bully who makes the lives of the slaves in the household (himself included) utterly intolerable. It's a first sign of an antagonism towards power that will later surface in his fables.

Because he has spoken out, the master decides to be rid of Aesop in case he ferments rebelliousness among the other slaves. Aesop is transported to Ephesus (in modern Turkey) and put up for sale. However, because of his appearance and his impairments, no one will buy him. He is shipped on to the island of Samos where a second attempt is made to sell him. At the market, Xanthus, a potential buyer and an eminent philosopher (whose existence can't be verified historically either), is visibly disgusted by Aesop's defects. Aesop, however, has a brilliant response to Xanthus's revulsion. A philosopher, Aesop says, should value a man for his mind rather than his body. Xanthus is impressed and perhaps chastened. He buys Aesop for his wife. He will be her manservant.

Aesop moves into Xanthus's home where he reveals himself to be a clever, shrewd, sarcastic, mercurial fellow: part trickster, part fool and a maverick who can untie seemingly intractable problems by the application of remorseless logic and reason. Here is a typical story from this period.

Xanthus must leave home and go somewhere, but he's anxious about what might happen on the journey. He sends Aesop outside to see if there are any crows around. According to popular belief, two crows are a portent of good fortune, while one crow is sign of bad luck. Aesop spots two crows outside and returns to Xanthus with the good news. The augury is good. He can make the journey.

Xanthus, delighted, throws the door open, steps out and sees ... a single crow. One of the pair that Aesop spotted has just flown away.

Xanthus aborts his expedition and rounds furiously on his slave. Aesop had reported two crows, says Xanthus, when in truth there was only one, and had he set off, as the omen foretold, he would doubtless have met disaster. To teach his slave to be more careful, Xanthus issues orders for Aesop to be whipped.

As Aesop is waiting to receive his punishment a messenger comes to Xanthus's house with a dinner invitation. Xanthus is delighted and accepts. When Aesop learns about this he realises that he can now stop his impending whipping because there is a glaring inconsistency in Xanthus's thinking.

Your omens, Aesop says to Xanthus, are the wrong way round. His good omen has ended in misfortune, while Xanthus's bad omen has ended in good fortune. He, Aesop, who saw two crows, an auspicious omen, will shortly be flogged like a dog, whereas Xanthus, who saw one crow, an inauspicious omen, will soon be making merry with his friends at supper. Clearly, the omens mean the reverse of what they're supposed to mean, which makes them meaningless. Aesop's argument persuades Xanthus. He scrubs Aesop's beating. The demolition of certainties through the ruthless exposure of internal contradiction, as here, will be one of the hallmarks of Aesop's fables.

After Xanthus (and possibly this has something to do with Xanthus's wife – perhaps she and Aesop are lovers), Aesop, still a slave, is passed on to Iadmon, a Samian. The latter, like Xanthus, is also impressed with Aesop. He grants Aesop his freedom. Aesop is now at liberty to forge an independent life. He becomes an adviser to the king of

Babylon and he helps the king win a battle of wits with the king of Egypt. Aesop is rewarded handsomely for his expertise and thereafter he becomes a fixer, adviser and helper to orators, tyrants and politicians. His numerous employers value many things about him but what they value most of all is his narrative capacity. When he acts for you Aesop doesn't simply make an argument or construct a case. He does something else. He tells stories – small, sharp fabular ones – and then, by the addition of a little addendum or moral (and the connections are ingenious), he interprets these stories in the interests of his clients. Typically, the morals have three parts experienced in the following order. The first is the italicised sentence before the fable, which announces what's coming, known as the promythium (Greek *pro-mythos*, 'before-story'). The second is the understanding expressed by the character inside the story, which shows what the character has grasped, known as the endomythium (Greek *endo-mythos*, 'inside-story'). And the third is the italicised sentence after the fable, which summarises the message of the story that's just been told, known as the epimythium (Greek *epi-mythos*, 'after-story'). Not all fables come with all three but all come with one or two addenda that bridge the gap between the fiction and the present moment. These meanings (the morals wrung from the text), at least when Aesop is in charge, are surprisingly local and particular as well as wonderfully clever.

For instance, acting on behalf of a demagogue on Samos who is on trial (if found guilty he will pay with his life), Aesop offers the following narrative in his defence to the court.

A vixen is crossing a river. She is caught by the current and washes up in a gully. The gully is deep and she can't get out. The sides are too steep. Besides being trapped, the vixen is also rotten with ticks. A hedgehog, who lives in the gully, offers to pick the ticks off her body. This won't help her to get out of the gully but at least it will mean she won't be tormented by tick bites any more. The vixen, however, declines the hedgehog's offer. The hedgehog is puzzled. He asks her to explain. Her ticks, she says, have been sucking away at her for ages, albeit there's almost nothing left for them to take at this point. However, if these ticks go, she says, they will be replaced by new ticks who will be hungry, aggressive and indefatigable. They will drink whatever blood is left in her body and she will die.

Using his fable as a springboard, Aesop then makes the following argument on the defendant's behalf. He likens the islanders to the old vixen and the demagogue on trial to one of the fat, engorged ticks stuck to her, adding that of course it's wealth not blood he's swollen with, the wealth of the people of Samos. The demagogue can be executed, Aesop concedes, but that will not be the end of the demagoguery. He will be replaced and the new demagogue will suck the people of Samos dry and then the people will find they are worse off than they would have been had they kept their old demagogue, which is exactly what the vixen understood. You're better off with familiar than unfamiliar tormenters. The old won't kill you, while the new will.

Aesop's technique (telling stories and then connecting them to the moment) is successful. He wins arguments for a lot of clients. His work also becomes ubiquitous. Listeners, having heard his fables, find they are compelled to retell them and as a result they spread. The effect of this combination of political success and literary reach is that Aesop becomes one of the best-known individuals in the world as it is in the fifth century B.C.

And then, he falls. He visits Delphi, the city with the famous oracle. Here, he disrespects the local aristocracy and the city's principal deity, Apollo. This isn't surprising. He's always been outspoken, pugilistic and ready to disparage vested interest and received opinion. The Delphians are outraged. They 'plant' a gold cup in his luggage. Then they 'discover' the cup. They accuse Aesop of stealing from the oracle's temple, a sacrilegious crime and a capital offence. He is brought to trial. In his defence, Aesop deploys several of his own fables with moral addendums. One of these is

'The Frog and the Mouse' (number 33 in the present collection). In this tale a frog and a mouse, who are tied together by twine, swim together in a pool. Then the frog dives, dragging the mouse down into the depths. The mouse drowns. The bloated corpse of the mouse floats to the surface, with the frog still attached. The mouse is seized and carried away by a bird of prey, and the frog, who is still tied to the mouse, is taken too. Both are then eaten. Aesop connects the fable to the predicament in which he finds himself in the following way. He's the mouse and the Delphians are the frog, he says, and he and the Delphians are tied like the mouse and the frog are. They can kill him but then they will die too because he and they are connected.

The court are not persuaded by this conceit. Aesop is found guilty. He is taken to the cliff where prisoners are executed and he is hurled to his death. Shortly after this, famine, pestilence and war beset Delphi. The Delphians consult their Oracle of Apollo and learn that their woes are the direct result of their mistreatment of Aesop and his unjust death. It turns out they were tied after all, just like the mouse and the frog. The oracle instructs the Delphians to make amends for their offence and the city builds a pyramid in Aesop's honour.

III

Aesop is first referenced by other writers in the fifth century B.C. In his history of the Greco-Persian wars, the Greek historian Herodotus describes Aesop as a historical figure from Thrace (the modern Balkans) who had lived on the island of Samos in the Aegean Sea, near the coast of modern Turkey.

In *The Birds*, Herodotus's near contemporary, Aristophanes, the comic playwright, has the character Pisthetaerus chide the Chorus Leader for his failure to go over his Aesop. Then he summarises the Aesop fable that the Chorus Leader would have known had he been across his Aesop. From the play text it's clear that Aristophanes is sure that everyone in the audience will agree with Pisthetaerus. Everyone who's anyone knows their Aesop.

The earliest surviving written collection of Aesop's fables is the work of Phaedrus: born a slave in Thrace in about 15 B.C., he moves to Italy, gains his freedom and produces his version (five books, ninety-four fables) in Rome. Phaedrus's version is notable for two innovations. They're written in verse and there's no 'inside-story' moral. Instead, Phaedrus relies on the morals appended top and bottom.

Many writers follow Phaedrus and produce their own version, often in verse. Aesop's fables also attract the attention of pedagogues who see that they can use the fables to teach grammar, rhetoric and, most importantly, morality. This is a huge change. In the ancient world, Aesop's fables are for adults and their morals aren't closed. They are open and endlessly varied. Speakers are free to repurpose the fables as occasion demands. But once the pedagogues get hold of Aesop, work which was once playful and ambiguous is remade into a tool for the inculcating of approved norms. This begins to happen in English with Caxton, and by the time we come to Roger L'Estrange's English translation, published 1692, with its foreword that states its explicit function is the initiation into children of 'Sense', the process is complete. Aesop, at least in English, is now the means by which moral absolutes are shoehorned into the heads of the impressionable young. And that idea that Aesop and moral instruction come as a package has been with us, more or less, ever since.

IV

Broadly speaking, Aesop has two subjects – the exercise of power and the experience of the powerless who endure life and all that it inflicts on them.

In his fables, the gods and goddesses who exercise power tend to be capricious, wilful, thoughtless and unforgiving, while the powerless, the mortals (many of whom are animals) who endure life and all that it inflicts on them tend to be blind, deluded, foolish and careless. The discrepancy between the powerful and the powerless is a source of humour but it is also the basis of Aesop's critique. The human world, as Aesop has it, is a place of rough justice, deep hurt, epic cruelty and unstinting monstrousness.

When we are in trouble, as we are today, we revert to the literature of the ancients. We do this because this literature seems more relevant than modern literary art. This is certainly the reason why we, who both loved Aesop's fables when we were children, have gone back to his work. His stories may be full of idiosyncrasies and impossibilities but the bitter truth lurking within the fables seems absolutely of the moment, of now – our rulers are detached and their subjects are suffering; life is unfair and justice is a fantasy. In the fables, as presented on the following pages with all their fabular integrity (speaking animals, thoughtful satyrs, capricious gods, et cetera) intact, we believe you will find the present. We hope this will be a salutary experience, and, who knows, perhaps it may even catalyse resistance or focus opposition to the present moment and to modern times.

The source of the fables that follow is Émile Chambry's *Ésope Fables*. Chambry has 358 fables in his collection. We have selected 190 of these: the ones that struck us as the ones that hurt the most. We have grouped these according to our own system and then rewritten them in new language. Our intention is they should be read by adults and not children. We understand and sympathise with the contempt bad morals have provoked, but we've opted to keep them in this version because not to keep them would violate the spirit of Aesop. It is our hope, however, that our morals, rather than trivialising, violating or undermining the fables, darken, extend and amplify them.

Carlo Gébler and Gavin Weston

PROLOGUE

The People and Their Pouches

'It's time to make the first people,' Prometheus announced to the gods, 'and fill the earth with them.'

'These creations had better be good,' said Zeus. 'I don't want the planet overrun by idiots.'

'Don't worry about it,' said Prometheus. 'They'll be great.'

Prometheus went out onto the slopes of Mount Olympus and dug down till he found the special dense red clay he needed. He built a kiln. He made charcoal. With pine twigs he fashioned human frames; half were wide-hipped and female, and half were narrow-hipped and male.

Next, he wet the clay and daubed layer upon layer onto the pine frames to make people with legs and feet, fingers and toes, hands and noses. He fired his kiln, he baked his figures. Once they were cooked, he breathed into their mouths and their substance became flesh. Their eyes opened and they stood up.

Just then, Prometheus heard footsteps. He turned. It was Zeus with a bundle of carrying-pouches: leather made, open at the top, with straps.

'What's with the pouches?' asked Prometheus.

'These,' said the great god as he threw them down, 'are a little something for your people. You're going to love them.'

'Really?' thought Prometheus. 'I don't think so.'

'Okay, people,' said Zeus. 'Ladies first.'

The woman closest stepped forward. Zeus took two pouches and hung one down her back and the other down her front.

'All the mistakes made by other people will go in the

front pouch,' Zeus explained. 'You'll want them there, of course, where you can keep an eye on them. And all your own mistakes will go in the pouch at the back. Well, you won't want to be looking at your own mistakes all the time, will you? Next ...'

The pouches handed out and the people dispatched, the two gods, finally, were alone.

'Wouldn't it have been better for people to have their own mistakes in front where they can see them and the mistakes of others behind?'

'No,' said the great god, 'it's much better they focus on what's wrong with everyone else and never see what's wrong with themselves, obviously. This way they'll be arguing non-stop, which will be hugely entertaining, plus, because they'll be fighting all the time, they'll never come together to challenge our right to rule. Never. I'm telling you, these pouches will be the saving of us gods.'

'The gorged wolf does more harm than the hungry one,' thought Prometheus. 'This has to be the worst idea ever.' He said nothing of course.

Meddling is the privilege of the powerful.

1

CAPRICE, ARROGANCE AND THE EXERCISE OF ARBITRARY POWER

1.

The Good and the Bad Things

The things on earth that did people good were followed everywhere by the things that did them bad, and everyone thought they were the same. But they weren't: they were different. And for the things that did good, being mistaken for the things that did bad was hateful. They wanted the confusion to stop, so they flew to Olympus to see what Zeus could suggest.

'Oh well,' said the great god, once they'd explained the problem, 'this is easy. From today, you'll live on Mount Olympus with me, while the things that do bad will live on earth. You'll never be confused with them again.'

And the great god was right: the things that did people good, because they were such rare and exotic visitors (it was a long way to the earth and it was a journey they rarely made), never again were confused with the things that did people bad.

Unfortunately, there was a downside: Zeus's scheme also guaranteed that for people life was one long round of misery, since they shared the planet only with the things that did them bad. Zeus didn't notice this, of course, but even if he had, he wouldn't have cared.

The crooked furrow is the work of the great bull.

2.

The Hawk and the Nightingale

The nightingale sat in the oak tree and sang her plangent, heart-troubling song.

A hawk passed overhead. First he heard, then he saw her. The hawk was hungry. 'I shall have this one,' he thought.

He swooped down and seized the little songbird in his sharp talons. He carried her to the ground and threw her down on her back. His plan – to kill and eat her.

Pinned down and looking up at the hawk, the nightingale said, 'I'm only a morsel. You'll still be hungry after you've eaten me. Wouldn't you be better to find a bigger, proper meal?'

'Ah ha!' said the hawk. 'Here we see most thoughts are wishes. Let you go in order to chase what I don't have? No way.'

He broke the little bird's neck with a hard blow from his heavy beak, split her up the front and tore out the first soft, red, bloody morsel …

Once he finished eating, the hawk wiped the blood from his beak using the corpse's downy stomach feathers. Then, feeling full and clean and dry, he stretched his wings and rose slowly into the sky to look for his next meal.

Only fools fling away a sardine in the hope of a tuna.

3.

The Cock and the Cat

The cat pounced and floored the cock, pinning him to the earth.

'You can't eat me,' said the bird, looking back at the cat's mouth, its wiry whiskers, its sharp, nasty teeth. 'Leave me alone. I've never harmed you.'

'Maybe you haven't hurt me directly,' said the cat, 'but you're still an affront. Look at the racket you make every morning, ruining everyone's sleep. No, you have to go.'

'But I'm supposed to crow like that,' said the cock, 'and get everyone up. That's my job.'

'All right then,' said the cat. 'What about the way you breed with your sisters and your mother? That's disgusting and absolutely sickening. No, you have to go.'

'But that's my job too,' said the cock. 'If I don't mate with them, then the hens don't produce eggs and that's what my master wants – eggs. I have to do it.'

'Listen,' said the cat, 'say whatever you want, I'm not going without my dinner. Not happening. An empty belly knows no law, you know.'

And with that she bit off his head and then she ate him.

He who does evil never lacks for an excuse.

4.

The Disappointed Fishermen

On the shore a group of fishermen flung their dragnet into the sea and then began to haul it out again.

It was hard work, for their net was heavier today than it had ever been at any time during all the years they'd worked together.

'I'm telling you,' said one of the younger, more excitable members of the team, 'I've got a good feeling about this. I'd say we've got a catch here that's going to make us all very rich.'

All the other fishermen agreed with him except the oldest. 'Since you don't know what we've actually caught,' he said, 'don't assume anything.'

In the event, the old fisherman was right, for when they finally got the net up onto the shore, they found that all they had were rocks – masses and masses of them.

'Oh no,' said the excitable one. 'There I was thinking we'd a bumper catch and look what it turns out we have. Well, to hell with the sea, I say, and to hell with the god who rules the sea as well. I'm done with fishing. I'm giving it up. Are you all with me?'

'You bet,' and, 'Yes, I am,' shouted the others with the exception, again, of the oldest.

'Hang on, everyone,' he said. 'You thought you'd a great

catch, then it turned out you'd only caught stones, and now you want to give everything up? Are you mad? You just lost the run of yourselves, and that doesn't justify turning your back on the life you've made. That's ridiculous.'

Nobody said anything but the old fisherman felt his co-workers were moving his way.

'Of course,' he continued, 'nobody likes feeling how you're feeling: first the elation because of what you think you have, then the let-down when you realise what you've actually got. But these feelings, they're easy to get rid of, you know.'

He picked up a pebble and showed it to everyone.

'See this?' he said. 'These are your feelings.'

He threw the pebble into the sea.

'And now they're gone, just like that. Bitter regrets because of your own stupidity, just throw them away. With today there is always tomorrow, you know.'

'Yes,' his listeners murmured, one after the other, 'good words, very good words. We should remember those words.'

So they remembered them and later they quoted them to other fishermen and soon every fisherman was saying, 'With today there is always tomorrow,' and throwing a pebble into the sea at the same time to make the point really clear.

Happiness and misery are not fated but self-sought.

5.

The Wood-Cutter and the Fox

Pursued by huntsmen, the fox bolted into the wood-cutter's yard. He found the wood-cutter himself standing there.

'Friend,' gasped the fox. 'There are huntsmen on my tail. I beg you, hide me …'

'This tree is hollow inside,' said the wood-cutter. He waved at a short, thick trunk. 'Get you inside. They'll never find you in there.'

'You're kindness incarnate,' said the fox, a wordy fellow,

as he wriggled in through the hole in the side, 'and my gratitude shall be eternal.'

Once inside, the fox looked back through the hole he'd got in by. He saw the huntsmen who'd pursued him traipse into the yard and walk up to the wood-cutter. They carried bows and arrows.

'Did a fox just run through here by any chance?' the chief huntsman asked the wood-cutter.

'A fox!' said the wood-cutter. 'What, here in my yard?' He pointed at the log inside which the fox was hiding and rolled his eyes. The fox saw this and crouched lower.

'Yes, a fox,' replied the huntsman blandly. 'We were on his tail and we thought we saw him run in here.'

'A fox,' said the wood-cutter, pretending to draw an imaginary arrow from an imaginary quiver and then firing his imaginary arrow at the hollow tree where the fox was hiding. 'No, I haven't seen a fox.'

The fox saw everything and understood the wood-cutter's meaning. Fortunately, the huntsman didn't understand. He just thought the wood-cutter was a bit strange.

'Oh well, not to worry,' he said. 'Mr Fox has given us the slip again. Never mind, we'll get him another day.'

He and the other hunters sloped off, and as soon as the yard was empty the fox clambered out of the hollow log and began to slink off in the opposite direction to the huntsmen.

'Hey,' the wood-cutter shouted after him. 'Haven't you forgotten something?'

'I don't think so,' said the fox.

'Yes, you have. You haven't said thank you.'

'There is one word,' said the fox, 'which may serve as a rule of practice for all one's life – reciprocity. Had you really tried to hide me, thanks would be due. But you tried to give me away. That's why I owe you nothing.'

The fox vanished.

'Ungrateful wretch,' the wood-cutter shouted, but the fox was too far on to hear.

The blessing of the evil genii are really curses.

The Frogs Who Demanded a King

6.

The Frogs Who Demanded a King

The frogs, having no king and living in anarchy, sent a delegate to Zeus.

'Please, great god,' he said, 'appoint a king to rule over us.'

The delegate hopped away and Zeus was left alone, fuming.

'Don't they understand that well-being and tranquillity are found in the moderation of their own desires?' thought the great god. 'No, of course they don't. So then they come to me and I have to sort their problem out. Lazy, good-for-nothing frogs ...'

He went out onto the slopes of Olympus and selected a tree stump.

'This'll teach them,' he said. 'There you are, frogs,' Zeus shouted down.

He hurled the stump towards the pond where they lived. It landed with a terrifying splash. The frogs were so frightened by the noise they all hid under the banks.

'There's a king for you,' they heard Zeus shouting. 'Enjoy ...'

Time passed. The frogs forgot their terror, crept from their hiding places and swam up to their new king floating in the middle of their pond.

'What kind of king is this?' said one.

'A very big king,' said a second.

'And a very silent king,' said a third.

More time passed. The new king still hadn't said a word. Some of the bolder frogs decided to hop up onto him and get a better look.

They clambered on to the stump but still nothing was said.

'This isn't a proper king,' said one frog finally. 'What kind of king allows his subjects to sit on his head? No, no, he won't do. Zeus will have to do better than this.'

They sent their delegate back to the great god.

'Zeus,' he said, 'that king you sent us does absolutely nothing except bob about in our pond. Please, send us a proper king who'll do what a proper king does and who won't let us sit on his head.'

'You want a proper king?' said Zeus. 'All right, I'll give you a proper king if that's what you want.'

And he dispatched a water-serpent who ate them all up.

The deepest hole is the one you dug.

7.

Aphrodite and the Lovesick House-Ferret

Before cats were common, people used ferrets to kill any rats or mice that came into their houses. The ferrets were long, wriggly, furry creatures with pointy noses and they were very good at this kind of work.

Now, in those distant times, it happened that a female house-ferret fell in love with a young man in her city who had lovely dark skin, shiny blue-black hair and a beautiful singing voice.

The house-ferret went to the goddess Aphrodite.

'I love him with all my heart,' said the ferret to the goddess, 'but he will never look at me, let alone love me – not as I am now, a mere ferret. However, if I was a girl, I'm sure he'd love me, and I know I'd love him back.'

The goddess found herself pitying this ferret. 'All right, I'll make you a woman,' she said and she turned the ferret into a woman with soft brown skin and black eyes.

When the young man saw the girl in the street of their city the next day he was smitten. She was so beautiful. He spoke to her. Her voice was so lovely, so smooth, so stirring. He decided on the spot they must marry. He proposed and she accepted, of course.

A priest married the pair, watched by an invisible Aphrodite.

'Her body has changed,' Aphrodite said to herself, 'but has her personality?'

The couple retired to the nuptial chamber and the goddess, determined to answer her own question, slipped in after them. She found them in the bed, naked under the purple sheets, consecrating their union.

Aphrodite conjured up a mouse and set it going. The little grey thing scampered across the bedroom's stone floor.

The bride, although in the midst of love-making, smelled its mouse scent and heard its tiny feet scratching as it ran – both irresistible to her.

'Mouse!' she shouted joyously.

She pushed her new husband off her, flung herself onto the floor and scampered after it, snapping her teeth. The mouse got under the bed. She was about to follow when the goddess materialised and put her foot on the bride's leg to stop her moving.

'I see you now for what you really are,' said the goddess to the naked bride. 'You might look female but inside you've a ferret's heart and I don't want this lovely young man wasting his life as your partner. You won't make him happy and he won't make you happy either.'

Aphrodite clicked her fingers and the new bride turned back into a ferret. She dashed under the bed and re-emerged a moment later with the mouse in her mouth.

'You won't want to thank me now,' said Aphrodite to the groom, 'but later you will.'

The goddess vanished and the ferret slipped away too.

You can change costume but not character.

8.

The Little Gudgeon, the Dolphins and the Whales

The dolphins and the whales were brawling on the sea's surface and in the depths their battling could be heard.

A little gudgeon swam up and poked his head out of the water. In every direction he saw dolphins and whales twisting, roiling, bleeding and biting, and he saw the sea was red with blood too.

'You'll have to make peace sooner or later,' the little gudgeon shouted in his tiny, piping voice at the fighting creatures, 'so why not do so now before one of you is killed?'

A blood-smeared dolphin, with bite marks up and down his back, heard the gudgeon and turned to him. 'I'd rather die than take advice from a minnow like you,' he said, 'and I'm sure all the other great fish up here will be of the same opinion. So stop interfering and get back down to the depths where you belong before I snap you in two ...'

By sunset, dead whales and dolphins were floating everywhere and crowds of squawking gulls came to peck out their eyes. Oh that the great had listened to the small gudgeon.

Ignorance is very much a voluntary misfortune.

9.

The Lion in the Cave and the Hind

The hind ran. The hunters who were after her were closing in behind.

The hind saw a cliff looming in front of her with a cave at the bottom.

'I'll hide in there in the dark,' she thought. 'The hunters won't see me. They'll run past. Then I'll come out and run back the way I came. I'll get away. I'll live.'

This seemed like a good plan. The hind darted in. The cave was damp inside and smelled of wet stone as well as something else, something meaty and troubling. Two eyes shone from the black at the back: bright, fierce and malevolent.

'Who's there?' said the hind. A low rumble came in reply. 'A lion,' she said. 'I've stumbled into his lair.'

She heard his pads on the cave's earthen floor as he hurtled towards her.

'I hid where I thought I'd be safe from men,' said the hind, 'and found it was home to something even worse than them.'

The lion would be on her in a second, she knew, and a second after her throat would be ripped and her blood would be gushing, and then she would be dead.

However securely you may climb, never say you cannot fall.

10.

The Bramble and the Silver Fir Tree

The prickly shrub and the coniferous tree were arguing as to which of them was superior.

'Seeing as I'm tall, slender and graceful,' said the fir, 'I'm obviously better looking than you; but I'm also more useful. The deck of every ship that sails is made of fir wood.'

'That may be so,' said the bramble, 'but if you gave a moment's thought to the saws and axes that are going to tear you down one day, you'd have to agree: better a bramble any day than a fir tree.'

In the fray the weak are strong.

11.

The Earth and Hermes

Zeus summoned Hermes.

'Prometheus's people down on earth,' began Zeus.

'Yes,' said the lesser god. 'What about them?'

'All they eat is what they scavenge or hunt and, not being very good at either, they're hungry all the time.'

'True,' said Hermes.

'I want you to go down and show them how to break

the ground, plant seeds and so on. Teach them how to feed themselves.'

Hermes flew to earth and gathered all the people together.

'Right, folks,' said Hermes, 'I'm going to show you how to grow your own food, and to do that the first thing you do is you dig over the ground. Watch.'

Hermes drove his spade into the ground.

'Ah, that hurts,' Earth shouted. 'What are you doing?'

'What do you think?' said Hermes. 'I'm showing people how to prepare the ground for planting, that's what.'

'I don't want them feeding themselves at my expense,' Earth shouted back. 'Take them away.'

'Sorry,' Hermes said, 'no can do. Zeus's orders. They must be shown how to grow food so they can eat.'

'Well,' said Earth, 'if Zeus insists, I can't stop you. Show them what to do, but don't you worry, I'll make them suffer. Oh yes. What smarts teaches, isn't that what they say?'

Life is an onion that one peels crying.

12.

Shame and Zeus

When Prometheus made the first men and women he gave them all sorts of inclinations but he forgot to include shame. It was an oversight Zeus knew he must remedy at once. Without shame they'd never be decent.

'Shame,' shouted the great god.

Shame appeared before the god. She was a small, thin naked girl with flaxen hair, about ten inches high.

'Listen,' said Zeus. 'Men and women, I've got to put you into them. They're never going to swallow you, so the only way in is through the rectum.'

'What?' said Shame. 'No way. I'll do anything but I won't do that.'

'Oh yes, you will,' said Zeus.

'Oh no, I won't.'

'Listen, I'm the god here. You do what I tell you. You're going in the back way. It's an order.'

'What if I go in the front way?' said Shame.

'That could work with the females,' said Zeus, 'but I don't think the males will wear it.'

Shame pondered. Perhaps she could barter her humiliation for something. But what? Then she had it.

'All right, great god,' she said. 'If I must I must, but it'll be on one condition.'

'Go on.'

'Eros …' she said.

Eros was Aphrodite's son and the inciter of all desire. Shame, seeing everything that Eros did as the opposite of her work, hated him.

'I'll do what you say but it's on condition Eros doesn't come in the same way, and if he does, that's it, I won't stick around, I'm buggering off.'

'Yes, whatever,' said Zeus. He just wanted her gone and the job done.

Shame went to earth and climbed in through one rectum after another to put shame into everyone. The job was just as vile and offensive as she'd imagined it would be, and then, to her great chagrin, she saw Eros was indeed charging after her, following her route in.

'I told Zeus I wouldn't stay if Eros followed me,' she said, 'and I won't. Let people do it that way and feel no shame. See if I care.'

'Ah, but,' said another voice in Shame's head. 'If you do absent yourself, think what'll happen. There'll be talk, won't there?' And then she imagined the talk. 'Isn't Shame supposed to make people ashamed? But she's not: they're not feeling any shame when they do it up the rectum, are they? No, they're not. And do you know why? Because she's flounced off, hasn't she? Well, I ask you … is it any wonder people behave in such a depraved way? Of course it isn't, and it's all Shame's fault. She ought to be ashamed of herself, running away like she has.'

The very idea that she was to be vilified for not shaming people filled Shame with, well, shame.

'Right, I'll do my shaming duties,' she said. 'I'll insert myself into every person. But, here's my price. I won't stop at one kind of love. No, whatever way they do it, whatever way love comes in – the front way, the back way, the mouth, any way – I'll afflict them with shame. I shall make love such a bitter weed. Oh, they'll suffer, and the more they suffer, the more Zeus will love me.'

The future Shame saw filled her with such joy that all the dark feelings that had clouded her mind a moment earlier vanished like a puff of smoke and suddenly she was perfectly and immaculately happy.

Just as the tongue always goes to the aching tooth, so shame always follows love.

13.

King Fox and Zeus

Zeus had been closely watching the fox for some time.

'He's so intelligent,' the great god said, 'and I like that a lot. But I also notice how supple his thinking is and I like that even more. The fox tries something. It doesn't work. Does he try again and again even though it isn't working like others I know? No, he doesn't. He recognises he's defeated and he walks away. He never gets stuck on anything. Oh yes, a remarkable fellow.'

Zeus paused and pondered. 'Well, it's obvious what I must do. I shall make the fox the king of the beasts. He deserves it.'

Zeus conferred kingship on the fox in a short ceremony

and, as he was doing this, an unwanted thought came to him. 'Will his elevation change him?' he wondered. He hoped not.

Time passed. Zeus remembered his niggle. Had it any substance? He looked down at the earth and saw King Fox being carried along in a litter by some of his subjects.

'So,' said Zeus, 'he thinks he's that kind of king, does he? Well, let's see if he can actually act like one.'

Zeus released a May bug right in front of the fox: it was large, chestnut in colour and made a loud and disagreeable whirring sound as it flew about the fox's face.

'Get away,' shouted King Fox. 'That's an order.'

But the May bug went on buzzing around the fox, and this made King Fox angrier and angrier. He was being ignored by a subject, who was a mere bug.

'If you don't go away, you're going to be sorry,' King Fox shouted.

The bug buzzed on.

'You're not listening are you? Right –!'

King Fox jumped up and snapped at the insect; he missed. The May bug zigzagged away.

'Come back,' shouted King Fox, 'and take your punishment.'

The May bug ignored King Fox. King Fox leapt off the palanquin and ran after him, snapping his teeth.

'Oi,' shouted Zeus, who had watched the whole scene.

King Fox froze. He knew Zeus's voice.

'A real king would never chase a May bug,' said Zeus. 'I hereby revoke your kingship. Henceforth, as before, you shall just be one beast among many.'

The palanquin carriers heard Zeus and tossed the palanquin aside.

'Well, now you're the same as us again,' one of the carriers shouted at the fox, 'you can walk the same as us.'

The carriers sloped off and the fox crept inside a rotten tree and wept bitter tears for the rest of the day.

The fortress surrenders from within.

14.

Apollo and Zeus

Apollo, a keen but also a competitive archer, approached Zeus.

'Which of us can fire his arrow farthest?' he said. 'You might say it's you but I say it's me. Well, there's only one way to decide. Let's see who can shoot the farthest.'

'I accept the challenge,' said Zeus.

The two gods went outside.

'You fire first,' said Zeus.

The lesser god drew his bowstring tight and loosed an arrow. As it flew away through the air, Zeus stepped forward from where they stood and, at the very instant Apollo's arrow buried its point in the ground on the far horizon, Zeus set his foot down beside it.

'With a stride like mine,' Zeus shouted back, 'why do I need to bother with how far I can shoot an arrow?'

A mere wolf should never step on the pack leader's tail.

15.

The Archive of Human Crimes

Zeus was getting confused.

'Hermes,' he called.

The lesser god stepped forward.

'There are too many people,' Zeus said, 'and they have too many faults. I simply cannot keep track of who's who and what they've done. I'm not just a god, I'm the great god, as we know, but even I, the great god, have my limits.'

'So what have you in mind?' asked Hermes.

'An archive of human folly,' said Zeus.

'Meaning what, exactly?' said Hermes.

'Well,' said the great god, 'the earth is full of broken earthenware and potsherds and what-have-you, which human beings just throw away, as is their wont, just like they shit and piss wherever they wish. Really, they are the most revolting species. So you will gather these potsherds – that'll make the place look tidier – and then you'll go round and each person will get their own bit of broken pot with their name and their faults written on it. And once you're done, you bring all the fragments back and put them in there.' Zeus waved at a big empty box that stood at the side of his throne. 'And then the next time I have to pass judgment on some miscreant I'll have their information at my side, easy to access, and I'll be able to dispense the right punishment because I'll know everything, won't I? Isn't that a brilliant idea?'

Hermes didn't think so. What would actually happen, he guessed, was Zeus would never match the potsherd to the person it belonged to because he hadn't the patience, and then he'd either end up punishing the wrong person, or he wouldn't bother doing anything because the whole palaver was too finagling. Fortunately, Zeus couldn't read his mind and Hermes knew better than to speak it.

'Yes, it's a brilliant idea,' he said.

The lesser god flew to earth and gathered all the bits of broken earthenware that were lying everywhere. Then he went round and he got everyone's name and their faults and wrote everything down. And when this great census of sin was done, he carried all the pottery bits back to Olympus and put them in Zeus's wooden box.

It wasn't long before the first name belonging to a miscreant on whom Zeus had to rule arrived. The man was languishing in a jail where he'd been put because he couldn't honour a debt. His name was Adam. A common name.

'Hermes,' Zeus shouted. The lesser god stepped up. Hermes would carry out whatever sentence he prescribed.

Zeus opened his box and began to rummage among the dusty, jagged shards. He found an Adam all right, but it wasn't the Adam who was lying in jail. It was another Adam and, according to the information on the potsherd, this other Adam had many faults – so many there was only one punishment.

'Go down to the jail and blind him,' said the great god.

'Really?' said Hermes. 'Is that absolutely necessary?' He knew this Adam, the one in the jail, and he knew the other Adam, the one with all the faults, who was not in jail. Of course he did. Hadn't he done the inventory? Hadn't he spoken to every person on earth? Hermes really did know everyone.

'I think this Adam that's in prison is a blameless fellow,' said the lesser god, 'and certainly not someone who deserves such a harsh punishment.'

'Listen, Hermes,' said Zeus. 'The way it works is: I check the details, I pronounce the sentence, you carry it out. Got that? So what did I say? Blind him. Got it? Go down and take his eyes out.'

There was no point arguing. The lesser god left to do the great god's bidding. By sunset the wrong Adam, whose only crime was that he couldn't honour a debt, was blind and the offending Adam was carrying on as if he had never done wrong at all, when of course he had.

And so it went. The new system worked exactly as Hermes had imagined. When Zeus had to pass judgment on some person and he opened his box and tried to find the shard with their name on it, sometimes he would find a shard with the same name and then pass judgment on the wrong person, or sometimes he couldn't find the name so he did nothing, in which case no judgment was passed at all. It was an absolute mess; the innocent were squashed while wrongdoers went unpunished. But that was the system, and though complaints about its injustice were bruited about (on earth they never stopped shouting about the unfairness of it all; people, as Zeus often observed, really did excel at whingeing and complaining), the great god would never admit there was anything wrong with his system. Of course not, because if the system was wrong then that meant the great god who had devised the system was wrong, and the great god was never wrong. On the contrary, he was always right and, what's more, he demanded all should show proper gratitude to him because he was always right.

And so it goes.

Having inflicted justice, the powerful then demand thanks.

16.

The Shellfish and the Dog

The dog was partial to eggs. If he found one he would pick it up gingerly between his teeth, throw it back onto his tongue, press it against the roof of his mouth to break the shell and swallow the lot.

One day the dog found himself on the shore by the sea. On the ground he saw something glimmering and white.

'What's that?' he said. 'It doesn't have the egg shape but it has its colour. That must be how eggs are down here by the sea.'

He took the shellfish into his mouth, failed to break it and swallowed it anyway. Before long he had stabbing pains in his guts.

'I thought it looked like an egg because I wanted it to be an egg,' he said, 'but it wasn't. The belly is always a stranger to reason.'

His stomach heaved. He retched. The pain was searing. He curled up on the sand. A fever came. Visions followed. Some hours later, when it was dark, he died.

Who knows much, mistakes much.

17.

The Vixen and the Lioness

The vixen and the lioness had both just given birth.

'Look at my litter,' said the vixen. 'Eight lovely cubs. But you, my dear, just a single cub.'

'Yes,' said the lioness, 'only the one, but not a fox, my dear, a lion.'

Worth, not quantity.

The Clever Lamb and the Wolf

18.

The Clever Lamb and the Wolf

The wolf was following the course of the little stream running down the hillside when he saw the lamb ahead. The little creature was by himself, his flock was nowhere to be seen and he was balanced on the bank, his head down, quietly sucking water up with his long, narrow mouth.

'I want you, little lamb,' the wolf said to himself, 'but as you're so young and small and inexperienced, I've got to come up with a reason to eat you. I can't take you just like that.'

This sort of thinking was typical of this wolf, who believed it was essential to be ethical, just as long as all decisions regarding what was right and what was wrong were his.

'So what can I come up with,' continued the wolf, 'as a reason to eat him?'

He pondered for a moment.

'Got it,' he said, his eyes brightening and widening.

The wolf sauntered up to his intended victim. 'Hello, little one,' he said.

The lamb looked up. The wolf was so close he knew at once there was no point trying to run.

'I've got some bad news for you,' said the wolf, 'and I'm just going to give it to you straight. I have to eat you. You've muddied the waters and that's what happens to animals who muddy waters. They get eaten. Simple as that.'

'What are you on about?' said the lamb, in his high, tiny voice. 'You've come from upstream and it's a physical impossibility that I could have muddied the waters up there. Water flows down not up. But even if you'd been below and come up, the water wouldn't have been muddy. When I drink I suck quietly and I don't stir the stream's waters when I do.'

The wolf nodded. All this, he had to admit, was true.

'Fine, you haven't muddied the waters,' said the wolf, 'I accept that. However, the fact remains, you're a nasty piece of work. Last year you said some vile things about my father and, as we know, if you slander you get eaten. That's the way it goes.'

'I wasn't even born last year,' said the little lamb. He was a quick-witted and nimble-tongued fellow.

'Oh, shut up,' said the wolf. 'Whatever you say in the hope of staying alive, I'm having you anyhow.'

He closed his jaw around the lamb's neck and bit down hard, snapping the creature's vertebrae and killing him instantly.

There is no defence against the unscrupulous.

19.

Zeus and the Asses

All day, every day, all over the earth, the poor asses, as they hauled burdens here, there and everywhere, were jabbed, stabbed, jerked, beaten and abused. Oh yes, it was hard being an ass ...

One evening the asses got together to discuss their lot. They agreed their lives were wretched and they nominated one of their number to petition Zeus on their behalf to ask they be released from bondage.

This delegate took himself to Olympus. He begged for and was granted an audience. He was brought before the great god.

From his throne Zeus studied the creature who had appeared in front of him. He had a dun pelt, a sagging back, ridiculous ears, stick-thin legs with knobbly knees and hideous gnarled hooves. He also had a distinct smell, a mix of earth and manure and ass sweat. All in all, the great god thought, he was a most unattractive creature.

'What do you want?' Zeus asked.

'We're worn out, us asses,' said the supplicant ass. 'People load us up with great weights that are far too heavy for us and then they shout, "Silly ass, on you go, you brute," and just to be sure we've understood their meaning, they strike our rump with a stick or yank the bridle so viciously the bit cuts open the sides of our mouths and our ass blood spurts out onto the road, dark and warm and red; and then we set off with our heavy load, and we keep on going, never stopping, our hooves aching, our bones hurting, our joints screaming, and as we go people carry on beating us with delight; and we don't stop until we've got to where we're supposed to go. It's grotesque, this life we lead as beasts of burden, and we beg to be released from carrying duties altogether.'

'Listen, you idiot,' said the great god. 'You're an ass. Do you know what that means? It means you're meant to carry. You *are* the beasts of burden. That's what asses are. That's what all you asses are. I made you to carry. You understand? And what you carry is whatever you're given. That's how it works and you don't get a say in this.'

'Oh, right,' said the supplicant ass in a quiet, emollient voice. He was a diplomat; that's why he'd been chosen. 'Of course, you're right. Yes, how utterly wrong to even ask that we be relieved from our carrying duties. I don't know what I was thinking. It would upset the balance of the world if the asses were suddenly excused carrying. It would set a precedent and then every animal would demand to be released from their duties and we couldn't be having that. Of course not. So how about this, great god: how about the weight that we are expected to bear is limited by decree?'

The great god pondered. 'If I issue a decree,' he said, 'like the one you want – you know, "Henceforth, all asses are only to carry so much. Break this rule and you will answer for it" – you know what's going to happen. People are going to go mad. You know what they're like! They love to complain when they believe some god-given right has been taken away from them. On the other hand, I do see how very hard are the lives that you asses live. Of course I do. Something has to be done. But we have to be cunning here. So, here's what I propose. Here you will see a great god at the top of his game. Pay attention.

'I will issue an edict. "The asses," it will say, "have a task to fulfil and, if they succeed, as their reward, they are to be released entirely from their menial role. No more carrying ever again."'

'Really?' said the ass. He could hardly believe he was hearing what he was hearing.

'Absolutely,' said Zeus.

'And what is it we have to do? What is this task that, once done, will mean we'll be released from carting and carrying for ever?'

'You have to produce a river of ass piss,' said Zeus. 'Make a river of your piss and you will never have to carry a burden ever again. That's what I will tell the world.'

The ass went back to earth and told the other asses.

'If we produce a river of piss,' he said, 'the great god will forbid people from loading anything on our backs ever again. We'll stop being beasts of burden and become creatures of leisure.'

'Well, what are we waiting for?' the asses clamoured. 'Let's get going.' They all pissed where they stood and they produced a considerable quantity of piss but no way did they produce enough to form what, by common consent, could be considered a river. But the asses were not disheartened. This was only their first attempt. They had a goal now – produce a river of piss – and to make that happen it was only necessary that they piss and piss and piss … So they got pissing. Whenever and wherever they stopped, they pissed. They became famous for it, for always pissing whenever and wherever they stopped.

Unfortunately, the asses never did manage to produce a river, nor did they hear the tinkle of laughter in the sky. Zeus and the other gods found the pitiful endeavour of the asses to piss a river endlessly amusing, but then, of course, it never did take much to make the gods laugh.

Nothing will shake our belief in what we desire.

20.

The Man and the Flea

The man woke in the dark and reached down to his calf. He found the small itchy bump and began to scratch.

'Bloody flea bite,' said the man. 'Bloody flea.'

He stopped scratching. It wasn't doing him any good; it wasn't giving him relief; it was making it worse. That was the thing about flea bites: they forced you to worry at them and you worried at them and that made them first swell and then, eventually, they burst and after they burst they bled, copiously. From something so little it was amazing how much misery ensued.

The man lay still and quiet in the dark. He felt something below. He was sure of it. Glancing, delicate, barely perceptible. The faint touch of the bouncing flea, traversing his knee, coming upwards, heading, he guessed, for the deep, humid, fleshy crease right at the top of the leg.

'Fleas love it in there,' he said inwardly, his lips staying still. 'And if the gods smile I'll catch you there, little flea …'

He let his knee fall outwards and his thigh roll up slightly, then got his hand into position right above the crease. He felt the tiny pest bouncing up his leg, tickling him faintly as it came. He waited. Finally, he felt it in the damp gulley at the edge of his groin.

'Yes,' he thought.

He darted his hand forward and snapped his fingers shut. A small wincing cry floated up in the darkness. He had it.

'Let me go,' said the flea.

'What?' said the man. 'You and your kind are a nightmare. You chew us up, your bites are frightful, they bleed, itch, ooze and torment us and still you shriek to be let go.'

'I'm asking politely,' said the flea. 'I'm not shrieking.'

'Well, you will be, I promise, when I kill you, as I will, seeing as all you do is cause misery and pain.'

The Man and the Flea

'But I can't help what I do,' said the flea. 'I'm a flea. I bite people. I suck their blood. I was made for that. And it's not that bad really, what I do, is it? Does anyone die? No. At worst, I'm just irritating. Come on. Flick me onto the floor. I'll hop off and, I promise, I'll never bite you again. Just let me live, please.'

'What, let you go so you can breed and make thousands more little monsters like yourself? Whether the harm you cause is big or small is beside the point. I want your sort eradicated. Quite simply, I refuse to share the earth with you, as you are completely and utterly pointless.'

The next bit was something the man had done before. He'd had lots of practice because over the years he'd dealt with lots of fleas. He manoeuvred the small ball up to his thumbnail, got it halfway over the nail and pressed down hard. At first he felt the insect's carapace holding and resisting, and then the creature's shell popped and a small smear of blood spread over his thumb and fingertip.

'Well done, you,' he said out loud.

He wiped the blood and the flea's body on the wall above the bed, turned on his side and went back to sleep.

No one loves justice like the executioner.

2

IRRECONCILABILITY, CONFLICT AND VENGEANCE

21.

The Vixen and the Eagle

Unlikely as it may seem, the vixen and the eagle became good friends; then, believing that if they were neighbours they would like each other even more, they decided to live side by side. To this end the eagle built a great dry nest at the top of a pine tree and hatched her chicks there, while the vixen made a snug den in the thicket at the tree's base and delivered a litter of cubs there.

One winter's day when the vixen was away foraging, the eagle, who also wanted food for her young, spotted the vixen's cubs playing at the foot of the tree. Her chicks were famished and there was nothing to eat for miles in any direction.

'I know we're friends, the vixen and I,' the eagle said, 'but there's nothing else for it. They'll have to be dinner. I'll have to take them ...'

The eagle dropped down, caught the fox cubs in her talons, flew them up to her nest and fed them, squealing and shrieking, to her fledglings.

At dusk the vixen returned and saw the bone splinters and the fur scraps scattered around the base of the tree.

'My cubs,' she shouted, 'my babies.'

The vixen looked up and saw her sometime feathered-friend sitting at the top of the tree in her nest looking cool, calm and haughty.

'She's fed my babies to her babies,' said the vixen. She boiled now not with grief but rage. 'I want to rip her to shreds,' she said. 'But she has wings and I don't. She's of the air and I'm of the earth. I can never get at her and so I can never punish her.'

The vixen let out a long anguished cry that the eagle

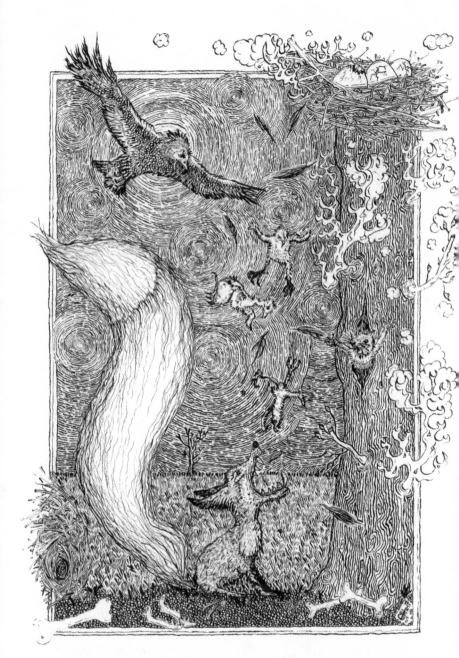

The Vixen and the Eagle

heard and recognised as the howl of pain the powerless make when the powerful betray them.

'Scream all you like,' the eagle muttered, 'it won't do you any good. I'm not listening …'

The next day, a hunter's camp nearby, a fire with a goat roasting on a spit, its discarded innards sizzling on the embers below … Flying overhead the eagle saw the lovely entrails and said, 'They'll make a tasty titbit for my babies.'

She swooped down and snatched them up, not realising that trapped in a kink in the intestine was a red ember, and flew them home.

'My darlings,' she said as she dropped the offal into the nest, 'something to feast on.'

The chicks began to tear the viscera apart. The ember fell from the fold that had held it and dropped onto the nest's floor, an amalgam of ancient bracken and brittle leaf, old twig and dusty moss: within seconds the nest, then the branch on which the nest sat and finally the whole crown of the tree were on fire.

Inside her den the vixen heard, coming from outside, the roar of the flames and the squealing and shrieking of the eagle's chicks.

'What's going on?' she said.

She rushed out, looked up and saw the mother eagle circling through black, thick resin-smelling smoke, and her eaglets, who couldn't fly, leaning out over the edge of their burning nest.

'Jump,' their mother shouted.

'Ah,' the vixen said, 'my time has come.' She tilted her head back and opened her jaws as wide as she was able.

The eaglets jumped, plummeted and plopped, one after another, straight into the vixen's wide waiting mouth. Then the vixen closed her mouth, savagely chewed and swallowed the pulpy, feathery whole in one great, greedy gulp.

Overhead the eagle let out a long anguished cry that the vixen heard and recognised as the howl of pain the powerful make when the powerless pay them back.

'Scream all you like,' the vixen said, 'it won't do you any good. I'm not listening …'

She wriggled into her hide where she planned to lie and wait for the enormous meal in her belly to digest.

Punishment is lame but it comes in the end.

22.

The Beetle and the Eagle

A high hot sun, an eagle in the clean blue sky and down on the stony plain below, which the eagle had her eye fixed on, a tiny brown moving dot.

The eagle dropped earthwards and the dot enlarged into a frantic, breathless, panic-stricken hare scurrying forwards, desperate to escape the bird of prey overhead whose shadow it could see floating and steadily expanding on the ground ahead.

And then the hare saw, just in front, flapping like a wet sheet when shaken, the shadow of the predator's wings that were beating just above and behind him. The eagle was getting closer while he was getting slower, with his heart hurting, his lungs aching, his body screaming.

'I can't escape,' cried the hare. 'Who will save me?'

'I will,' replied a fat glossy scarab beetle who, from under a rock, had been watching everything.

The exhausted hare flopped down in front of his would-be protector. The eagle floated in, talons outstretched, ready to kill.

'Stop right there,' said the beetle to the eagle. 'Let the hare alone – he's too weak to run another step. Different story, I grant you, if he'd a sporting chance of getting away, but look at him. I mean, it's just not fair to catch and eat him now, not when he's like this. He can't run another step.'

'Throughout my life,' said the eagle, 'I've made it a point of principle never to listen to small, pointless non-entities like you and I don't intend to start now.'

She broke the hare's neck, sliced his pelt open with her sharp beak, pulled off a strip of lovely warm flesh and gobbled this down.

'Fools never know how to be merciful, do they?' said the beetle. 'Well, fool, I'm going to teach you. You're going to be sorry you ever met me.'

From that day on the beetle searched out this eagle's nest and, once she had laid her eggs, he would push them out of the nest and they would smash on the ground.

After six years of this and not one chick hatched, the eagle fled to Zeus to whom she was sacred.

'I'm being harried by a lunatic,' she said. 'Every time I lay, this scarab comes and pushes my eggs out of the nest. I've not reared one chick in six years. You've got to help me.'

'You can nest on my lap,' said the god. 'The wretch won't be able to roll your eggs off my thighs.'

But the wretch had other ideas. As soon as the eagle laid, he made a big wet dung pellet, flew it to Olympus and dropped it over the great god. It landed on his lap. Disgusted, Zeus stood up without thinking to shake it off, and no sooner had he done this but the eagle's eggs rolled off and smashed on the floor. So this was now the seventh year in a row this eagle had failed to breed.

After this the eagle realised her only option was to change her habits. So she made it her business never to breed when beetles were in season – and thank goodness, for if she hadn't there wouldn't be any eagles alive today.

A great bend must have a great straightening.

23.

Aesop in the Boatyard

Aesop, teller of fables, was passing a boatyard where men were building boats.

'Here he is,' the boat builders shouted out, 'the great

Aesop in the Boatyard

Aesop. All day, every day, all he does is wander about dreaming up tales. He never does a tap of real work, does he?'

Aesop heard all, stopped and said, 'Pay attention, gentlemen. I'm going to tell you a story.'

The workmen went quiet.

'In the beginning there were two elements – chaos and water. Then along came earth, and Zeus told her to swallow the sea three times. She swallowed once and made the mountains. She swallowed a second time and made the plains. And when she swallows the sea a third time, which she has yet to do, you lot will be out of a job. I, on the other hand, will go on telling stories and being paid for them, including the story of your sorry end …'

Who blows into the fire will have smoke in his eyes.

24.

The Partridge and the Cocks

A bird fancier brought a partridge home to live with his cocks. All through the first day his cocks chased after and pecked at the new arrival ceaselessly. That night, when she got her first moment of respite, the partridge said to herself, 'I know why they hurt me. It's because I'm not like them. I'm an alien and that's why they hate me.'

The next morning she saw the cocks fighting ferociously among themselves and making each other bleed. The sight of red spurting down their feathered breasts brought to her mind the words of an owner she once had: 'He who treats you as he treats himself does you no injustice.'

'Well,' she said, having remembered this phrase, 'I'll never feel sorry for myself again, not seeing these cocks are as vicious to each other as they are to me.'

He who sleeps in a pond wakes up cousin to the frogs.

25.

The Quarrel

Two men, both competitive and argumentative, were arguing.

'Herakles is the greatest god,' said one. This man was a Theban and Herakles was the patron of his city.

'Rubbish,' said the other. 'Herakles spent time as a servant, which Theseus never did, and that makes him the greater of the two. Any idiot knows that.' This man was an Athenian and Theseus was the patron of his city.

The argument, following these lines, ran on for some time, and the two gods, both thin-skinned deities as it happened, heard the men quarrelling.

'How dare he say Theseus is better than me,' said Herakles.

'How dare he say Herakles is better than me,' said Theseus.

To teach the men a lesson, Herakles destroyed Athens, home of Theseus's champion, and Theseus destroyed Thebes, home of Herakles's champion.

In this way both mortals lost their nations. Of course the gods were delighted with the justice they'd meted out.

The tiger and the buffalo fight; the reeds and bulrushes die.

26.

The Killer

A man killed another man and ran. The parents of his victim chased after him.

The murderer reached the River Nile. He wanted to swim across but he couldn't get in because there was a huge wolf on the bank at the only spot where he could enter the water.

The man climbed a tree by the river's edge with the idea

of hiding there until the wolf left. He hadn't been up there long when a huge serpent, whose home the tree was, came slithering along a branch towards him, its tongue forking ahead.

Desperate times call for desperate measures. From the tree the man launched himself into the Nile.

The wolf on the bank heard the splash the man made as he entered the water. He turned. There was a crocodile in the shallows, and the wolf saw the monster snap to life and submerge. A moment later the wolf saw bubbles and some blood and he knew the crocodile had caught the man from the tree, had dragged him down to the bottom and at that moment the poor fellow was probably already dead.

He who builds underground is never far from Hell.

27.

The Poor Man

The poor man fell ill and, as death closed in, he promised the gods he'd sacrifice a hundred oxen to them if they let him live.

The gods had no need of the sacrifice, but they were curious to see if he would keep his vow or not – or, anyway, this was what they told themselves. They made him well.

'What are you going to do about your promise to the gods?' his wife demanded once he was back on his feet. 'You don't have a hundred oxen.'

'Don't worry,' he said, 'I have a cunning plan.'

He modelled a hundred oxen out of brown beeswax, adding little scraps of bone for horns and painting on black eyes. Then he carried his figures to the altar and threw them onto the fire burning there, and as they melted he called out, 'Oh, ye great and all powerful gods, receive this votive offering of a hundred oxen in discharge of the vow I made.'

The gods were unimpressed with this ploy and

determined to pay him back. They sent him a message in a dream: he was to go to the beach near his home, where he would find a thousand gold pieces.

The man woke and ran straight there. Unfortunately, he found not the gold but a group of pirates who'd been primed by the gods to expect him. The pirates seized the man and carried him off to Egypt where they sold him as a slave. And their asking price? A hundred oxen on the nose, of course.

If strokes are good to give, they are good to receive.

28.

The Vine and the Hind

The hind ran, a pack of hunters following. She came to a vineyard with vines in rows, their foliage thick and green and lustrous.

'I'll hide here,' said the hind. She dashed in and got under a vine where she knew she couldn't be seen. 'I'll be safe here.'

She caught her breath and then realised she was hungry.

'I might as well eat something while I'm here,' she said.

She began to nibble: one vine leaf and then another and then a third …

The hunters couldn't see her but one did notice a vine moving slightly. 'I bet that's where she is,' he said to the others.

All the hunters fired their arrows at this spot and one tore into the hind's shoulder. She sank down, blood sheeting the grapes that hung around her.

'The tree says to the axe, "You could not cut me if I had not given you the handle,"' she said, 'and if I hadn't eaten the vine and given myself away, it'd be hiding me still.'

We are often shot with our own arrows.

29.

The Water Snake, the Adder and the Frogs

The water snake lay floating in the pool where she lived.

She watched the adder slide to the water's edge, lower his head and suck water into his mouth.

'What are you doing drinking here?' the water snake said. 'I haven't given you permission. I've never given you permission. You come here day after day, and day after day I tell you – go somewhere else. This belongs to me. This is my water.'

'No, it isn't,' said adder. 'You can't own a spring any more than you can own a tree or a cloud. It's part of the world. It belongs to us all.'

'That was very well put,' said a frog who was watching quietly. This frog was one of the colony who lived there. He and the other frogs hated and feared the water snake, who they knew would have no qualms about eating them all.

'I'll tell you how we'll settle this,' said the water snake to the adder. 'Come tomorrow at this time and we'll fight – the winner gets the spring and may the best serpent win.'

'This could change everything,' said the same frog who'd spoken before. 'The adder wins, we get a new master. Think what that would mean? It would be a revolution. I propose to tell this adder that we'll take his side – if you agree, that is. That way, when he wins, if he wins, he'll be kind to us. What do you say?'

The whole colony agreed with the proposal. The proposer hopped after the adder and stopped her.

'I just want to tell you,' he said, 'that the frogs of the spring are with you. We want you to win and in the coming battle we'll weigh in, I promise.'

The next day the adder returned and battle commenced. At first the adder was out-fought by the water snake, and the frogs, who were watching, croaked loudly to spur the adder on, but they didn't join the fight for fear of what would happen if the water snake won. Later, the situation turned:

the adder proved the better fighter and the water snake was beaten and driven away.

'Well fought, that adder,' the frogs shouted. 'We always knew you were a winner …'

'Well, if it was so obvious I was,' said the adder, 'why then, having promised to take my side, didn't you join the fight? Things promised are things due, after all.'

'Ah,' said the frog who had pledged the colony's support. 'Frogs don't help with their arms and legs. They never get physical. I thought you knew that. They only help with their voices.'

The smaller the heart the bigger the tongue.

30.

The Dog and the Gardener

The gardener owned a dog; he was a wayward, incautious animal, much given to wandering. One day the gardener noticed he was missing. He whistled and he heard his dog barking back. He followed the sounds to the abandoned well at the bottom of the garden, peered in and saw his dog paddling about in the brown, muddy water at the bottom.

'How on earth did you get in there?' said the gardener.

The dog whined.

'I understand,' said the gardener. 'I'll get you out.'

He fetched a ladder and climbed down. At the bottom he got off the ladder and into the water. He could feel the silty well bottom between his toes. The dog growled.

'What's that for?' said the gardener. 'I'm here to get you out.'

He reached forward to grab the dog under his front legs and lift him up. The dog, fearing he was to be pushed under, snapped at his hand.

The gardener looked down: puncture marks and blood bumping over his knuckles.

'Wretch,' said the gardener. 'Well, you can get yourself out if you're going to be like that.'

He climbed back up the ladder and went to the water trough where he washed the blood off. He heard the dog barking as he did.

'He wants to die,' he said, 'let him. I'm not bothered.'

Every stone you throw at your neighbour's roof will fall upon yours.

31.
The Fox and the Old Lion

The lion woke in his lair, a deep, dark, dank cave. He did a swift audit of his body. His jaws ached, his paws ached, his joints ached, his eyes ached; and everything else ached too.

'There's no point denying it,' the lion said. 'You're too old to run around after prey. Your hunting days are done. You still have to eat, though, and there's only one way to manage that. Trickery. Pretend to be ill and eat your visitors.'

He saw a sparrow hopping about in front of his cave. 'Hey, sparrow, go spread the word. I'm sick but I'm happy to receive visitors. Go … tell the animals.'

Over the following months, one caller after another who came to the lion's den to commiserate was trapped, killed and eaten, but only the fox realised what was happening. One day he passed the cave and stopped at the entrance.

'You're sick, I gather,' the fox called in.

'Yes, rather poorly,' said the lion, speaking from inside.

He spoke in a thin, croaky voice, the sort of voice, thought the fox, that the lion would put on if he was pretending to be sick.

'Why don't you come in and show your face?' continued the lion. 'I could do with some company. It's lonely lying in here day after day, I can tell you.'

'I won't come in, thank you,' said the fox.

'It's just old age,' said the lion. 'It's not contagious, you know.'

'It's not catching something that worries me,' said the fox, 'it's something worse.'

'Really?' said the lion with what sounded like fake surprise.

'Yes,' said the fox. 'I see a lot of footprints out here leading up to your cave, but I don't see any leading away.'

The rose has thorns only for those who would gather it.

32.

The Fox, the Ass and the Lion

The fox, the ass, and the lion came to an understanding: they would hunt together. This was an unusual arrangement as they had never been allies before; furthermore, the ass did not eat meat. But there we are; they made an agreement and together they sallied forth to hunt as a pack.

Their expedition prospered: throughout the day they ran together and they caught and killed a lot of game. Then came evening. It was time to divide their spoils.

'You do the divvying up,' said the lion to the ass. His tone was quiet, even avuncular.

'I wonder if he's beginning to like me,' thought the ass.

He divided the meat into three perfectly equal piles. He didn't want the other two to find fault with his actions and for the pact then to fall apart.

'How about that?' said the ass. 'I think that's fair.'

'No, it isn't,' said the lion. He jumped on the ass's back, wrestled the creature to the ground and bit savagely into his neck. The ass was completely unable to take any evasive action, as he'd no idea this attack was coming, and he was dead within a few seconds and eaten within half an hour.

'Very tasty,' said the lion, standing up from the ass's remains, his bloody bones, his torn pelt, his trotters and his

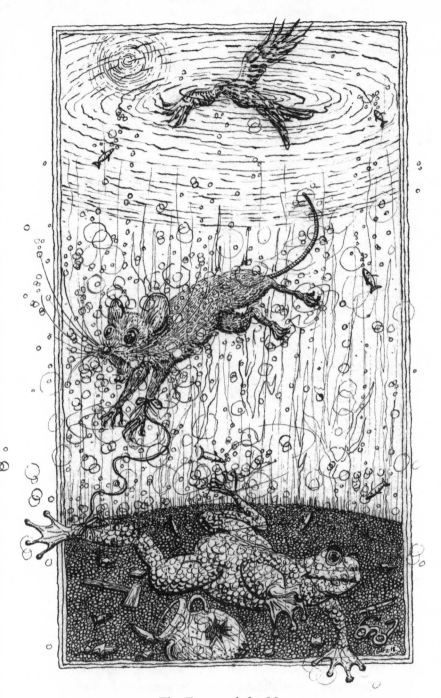

The Frog and the Mouse

head. The fox was still there. He had watched the whole scene.

'I'm glad to see you're still here,' said the lion. 'You aren't upset, are you?'

'I didn't see anything I haven't seen before,' said the fox.

'So, would you care to divide today's spoils?' said the lion. 'Now that it only has to go two ways, there'll be much more for both of us.'

The fox put a couple of mice into one heap and the rest of the prey into another heap.

'Mine's the mice,' said the fox. 'The rest is yours.'

'I say,' said the lion, 'who taught you to divide spoils so well? You really have done an absolutely brilliant job, you know.'

'Well, I got all my technique from the ass,' said the fox. 'His misfortune was my education.'

As the music, so the dance.

33.

The Frog and the Mouse

The frog was a bulky creature with a lovely brown and gold pattern on his body and heavy, thick back legs. One day he was sitting in a shaded damp spot on the edge of the lane near his home pond when a mouse scurried by. The mouse was a small grey creature, with a thin tail and tiny paws.

The frog struck up a conversation with the mouse. The frog's personality was dominant. He was an animal who always led. The mouse was submissive and always followed. These differences of character allured them to each other. Of course. They became friends. And thereafter, they knocked around together incessantly.

One day, after they'd been intimates for a while, the frog said, 'Have you ever thought how frightful it would be if we lost one another and then couldn't find each other again?'

'I have,' said the mouse. The thought had crossed his mind.

'Well, I've an idea,' said the frog. 'See this bit of string?'

'Yes,' said the mouse.

'What about we tie your front paw to my back leg. That way we'll be able to move around separately but we'll never lose contact.'

'Inspired,' said the little mouse, twitching with excitement. 'Here's my paw. Please, tie the knot …'

An autumn day, cold and bright. The frog and the mouse, joined by the string, went to a corn field. The grain had been cut and hauled away but here and there, among the stubble, were stalks that had been missed. The pair scavenged and found grains and ate these.

'Come to the pond,' said the frog, when both had eaten enough and were feeling full.

They left the field and, hopping and scurrying, and with lots of stops to untangle the string when it got caught, they got to the pond. It was black and wide and smelled vaguely of rot.

'Hey ho, and in we go,' said the frog. He jumped in and the mouse was pulled in after him. Then the frog plunged down into the pool's depths, dragging the little mouse behind. It had always been his plan when he suggested the string idea to drown the pliant, gullible little mouse one day. The mouse, of course, had had no idea what was coming and now, as he was pulled deeper and deeper, he panicked, squealed and struggled. It was all useless. He gulped, unable to breath, and great mouthfuls of water filled his tiny lungs. And before very long, without air, he died …

The mouse's bloated body floated to the surface. A kite, cruising over the pond, saw the corpse. The kite swooped down, seized the mouse and rose, the mouse in his claws, the wet string stretching from her leg and, at the other end of the string, which was fastened round his back leg, the frog, croaking with terror, as he was lifted into the air …

The kite dropped her prey at the edge of a field. The frog tried to hop away but, being tied fast, he eventually reached the end of the string and could get no further. The kite, seeing the frog was still alive and likely to drag the mouse away, jumped on him and drove her beak deep into the back of his head and killed him. The kite then ate the two tied bodies.

To deceive another greatly is to deceive oneself more.

34.

The Bear and the Travellers

A track through the forest with two travellers tramping quietly along it. It was afternoon and the sun slanted sideways through the trees, silvering the trunks and shining between the leaves. There was a rot smell and no birdsong.

In the distance, someway ahead, the bear loomed out from behind a tree and began to run at the two men. One man, he was athletic and agile, grabbed the branch of a tree that, by good fortune, was directly above him and hauled himself up.

'Hey,' the second, a heavier, stouter fellow, shouted after the first. 'Can you –?' He didn't finish the sentence. The pull-up he'd hoped for, the stout man realised, would not to be forthcoming, for the other man, clearly, was focused only on his own safety.

The stout man cast about. Where could he go? What could he do? How could he save himself from the bear hurtling towards him?

He saw a hollow at the side of the track. It was his understanding that bears never touched carrion and only ate what they actually killed. 'I'll lie in there and pretend to be dead,' he said to himself.

The stout man threw himself into the hollow's bottom face downwards. The bear bounded up. He peered up at the higher reaches of the tree that the first traveller had climbed but he couldn't see the man because he was high up and well screened by thick, dense foliage.

Then the bear ambled over to the second man, the stout one, who lay in the hollow hardly breathing, his whole body tight and rigid as if dead. The bear dropped his heavy head and sniffed the shoulders, the neck and finally the ears, one after the other, of the pretend corpse.

The stout man smelled the bear's bear smell, a deep meaty odour with honey and rotting fish and leaf mould in it, and he heard his breathing, deep and terrifying, and he felt his hot bear breath playing first on one ear and then the other. Then the man sensed the breath wasn't there any more, and he heard the sound, which came to him through the earth, of the bear's footfalls as he lolloped off.

'It worked,' the man said to himself. 'He thought I was dead.'

Still he didn't move. He counted to ten. He counted to twenty. He counted to a hundred. He heard the sound of a twig snapping, followed by that of the other man landing on the track, having jumped from the bottom branch of the tree he'd been hiding in.

'You're safe,' he heard the other shout. 'He's gone. We did it.'

The man in the hollow sat up. The other was looking at him.

'I saw it all,' the other said, 'from where I was sitting, up there.' He pointed at the tree up which he had hid. 'He spent a very long time, that bear, with his nose to your ears. What was he saying? Anything interesting?'

'Yes,' said the second man. 'He said, "Don't travel with those who, at the first sign of danger, flee and don't think to help you." That's what the bear said.'

Long are the dregs of an ill-deed.

35.

Horkos, the God of Oaths and the Man

A man was given a large sum of money by a friend to keep safe while he went away on a long journey.

Several years passed and then the friend returned from

his travels. The friend asked for his money, but the other had spent it all and said, 'What are you talking about? You never gave me any money to look after. You just think you did because something happened to your head while you were away. You got a knock or something and that's why you're imagining something that never happened.'

The returnee went to the court-house and raised a summons to compel the other to swear on oath he had never agreed to hold his money while he was away. The man got wind of this. The news made him feel queasy and panicky. To steal money was one thing, but to swear under oath that he had never been given the money to hold in the first place, as the summons would require him to do, this was something else. It would provoke Horkos, the god of oaths, who had a fearsome reputation when it came to punishing oath breakers, and when Horkos found out, as he would – he always did – Horkos would drag him to the cliff just outside the city and hurl him onto the rocks sticking out of the sea, far, far below, which was how he punished oath breakers.

'I can't stay in this city any more,' the man said to himself. 'I'll have to go somewhere else so I don't have to swear the awful oath, and I'd better go now.'

The man pulled on his cloak and scurried to the city's gateway, and there he met a man with a limp who, like himself, was heading out of the city.

'And who are you?' he asked.

He had a notion that this lame stranger, if he was interesting, might be good company for him on the road.

'I'm Horkos,' said the other, 'the god of oaths.'

'And where might you be going?' said the man.

'Well,' said Horkos, 'I'm leaving here and I'm going out into the world to seek out the ungodly who tell lies under oath or break their oaths.'

'And how long before you'll be back then, here in this city?' asked the man.

'Thirty years,' said Horkos, 'forty, even. Who knows?

There'll be plenty to keep me busy out in the world.'

'Right,' said the man, 'and good luck to you.'

'What?' said Horkos. 'You've changed your mind? You're not leaving?'

'No,' said the man. 'I thought I was but now I realise I don't need to.'

Horkos sallied out of the gate and the man went straightaway to the court-house and swore, without hesitation, that he had never been entrusted with the safekeeping of any money by his friend.

The following morning, just before dawn, the man was woken in his bed by a hand shaking his shoulder roughly.

'Come on, out of bed, we're going for a walk.' It was Horkos.

The god marched him through the city's empty streets, through the gate where they'd met the day before and towards the cliff. He could hear the sea in the distance beating against the rocks that he was about to be thrown onto.

'Yesterday you said you wouldn't be back for thirty or forty years,' the man said. 'But since I swore my false oath not even twenty-four hours have passed. You lied!'

They reached the edge of the cliff. The sea below was white and furious; the rocks sticking out of the sea at the foot of the cliff were black and monstrous.

'I didn't lie,' said Horkos. 'I only came back because you provoked me. You see, once I'm angry, I have a habit of returning straightaway.'

He pushed the oath breaker.

'That should have been obvious to you,' Horkos continued, but the man, already falling, already screaming, his cloak flapping fiercely, didn't hear.

He who breaks his word by it will be broken.

36.

The Father and His Daughters

The father, a widower, had two daughters. They were married together at a double wedding, the older marrying a gardener and the younger a potter.

Time passed. The man thought he'd visit his daughters and see how married life was treating them. He went to the elder one first.

'How are things with you?' he asked.

'It's all good,' she said. 'No complaints. The only thing we lack is rain. We need a lot of it for all the veg my husband's growing. In fact, we're praying for a month of it, nothing but rain, rain, rain, and it would be marvellous if you would join us.'

Her request had made him nervous: he had an instinct that if he agreed it would lead to conflict. 'I can't stay now,' he said. 'I've promised to be at your sister's.'

He went to see his younger daughter then.

'And how are things with you?' he asked.

'It's all good,' she said. 'No complaints. The only thing we lack is sun. We need a lot of it to dry all the pots my husband's made. In fact, we're praying for a month of it, nothing but sun, sun, sun, and it would be marvellous if you would join us.'

His intuition at his older daughter's had been right.

'Sorry, I can't stay,' he said.

'Are you going to see my sister?' his younger daughter asked.

'No, I saw her already.'

'What's the rush then? Why don't you stay?'

'No, I won't,' the father said. 'Now I've seen both my lovely girls, I'll be quite happy on my own at home for a while seeing neither.'

And he rushed home vastly relieved that he hadn't had to join either in prayers against the other.

Do not choose between two opposite ventures when you need both to succeed.

37.

Hybris and Polemos

Zeus was fed up with the way all the gods and goddesses carried on, and with how they had endless affairs and endless children but never settled down and lived proper pious, exemplary lives. What he needed, Zeus decided, was a family-friendly Olympus that would, in turn, set an example to the people on earth who also had endless affairs and endless children but never settled down and lived proper pious, exemplary lives.

The great god summoned all the deities before him.

'Everyone is getting married,' said Zeus, 'and to make it absolutely fair, you're all going to be paired by lot. Whoever fate decides you're going to marry, that's who you're going to marry, and that way none of you will be able to come running to me snivelling and whining later, saying, "Boo hoo, I'm unhappy with who I've got hitched to." Fate is deciding this, you see. She is our mistress of matrimony.'

The lots were drawn and all the gods and goddesses were assigned to one another until, at the end, only two were left and, of course, they didn't need to draw lots for there was no one for either to marry except the other. One was Hybris, the goddess of wanton violence, and the other was Polemos, the god of war. They were perfectly suited, as fate knew they would be, and no sooner were they spliced but they fell madly and utterly and totally in love, so much so that thereafter wherever he went, because they had become absolutely inseparable, she went too, thus doubling people's miseries.

The supreme talent of the powerful is always to make it worse.

38.

The Huntsman, the Horse
and the Wild Boar

The horse and the wild boar shared a meadow. The grass was rich and sweet and there was a small pond ringed with rushes for water and a stand of trees for shelter. It was a perfect spot, but unfortunately the relationship of the two creatures had been worsening for ages and had now reached boiling point.

'You're a menace, you know,' the horse said to the boar. 'You churn up the ground by rooting in it with your tusks, and you pollute the pond by washing your muddy body in it. If you were here on your own, that would be one thing, but you're not. We're sharing this field. Please, show some consideration. Don't do this anymore.'

'Look,' the boar said. 'You don't like me rooting, you don't like me wallowing – tough. I'm a boar, that's what I do. It's my nature. I can't change what I am. If you don't like it, go somewhere else.'

'Well, if he won't listen,' thought the horse, 'then he'll have to be taught a lesson. He won't like it but he's asked for it ...'

Soon after this conversation, the horse accosted a huntsman.

'I share a piece of ground with a boar,' said the horse. He described their life together.

'And what's this to do with me?' said the huntsman.

'I want to pay him back,' said the horse, 'put him in his box. Will you help me?'

'I will,' said the huntsman, 'but only if you help me back. We have to work together on this if we're going to succeed.'

'Go on,' said the horse. He feared where this might lead, though he also knew that if he was going to humble and humiliate the boar he would have to pay a price.

'It's not much I'm asking for,' said the huntsman. 'You just have to wear the bridle and the saddle and carry me on your back. You do that, then we can fix the boar together.'

'All right,' said the horse.

The huntsman put the tackle on the horse, mounted and rode him to the meadow. He caught the boar with a rope and then brought both animals back to his yard and tied them up. The boar he butchered: he salted the meat and it fed him and his family through a whole winter. The horse he kept and rode for years, and most days he liked to exercise the horse in the very meadow where the horse had once lived.

'It's looking good, don't you agree?' the huntsman would say as they trotted around. 'No churned up ground and clean, clear water in the pond.'

The horse, for his part, would have given anything to have back the life he'd had. What had he been thinking?

He who stirs poison will taste it.

39.

The Snake and the Wasp

The snake lay in the sun by the side of the road sunning himself. The wasp was nosing around and buzzing a bit too close to the snake for the snake's liking.

The snake hissed.

'No one hisses at me,' said the wasp.

He alighted on the snake's head and drove his sting through the snake's skin.

The startled snake recoiled with pain and hissed again.

'No one hisses at me,' the wasp said. 'Didn't you hear?'

The wasp stung again and again and again, while the startled snake shook, writhed and hissed in fury, throwing itself this way and that without ever managing to dislodge the wasp.

A donkey cart appeared with iron-bound wheels. When it was level with him, the maddened snake threw himself in front of the wheel closest. The iron rim rolled forward, flattening the wasp and splitting the snake's head. The cart passed. A kite above saw the carrion, descended and ate both.

Beware of him who has nothing to lose.

40.

The Ants and the Cicada

Winter. It rained for nine days and the wheat in the ant's storehouse grew damp. On the tenth day the rain stopped and the sun shone and the ants carried their grains from their store and laid them out to dry.

A hungry cicada saw the ants and what they'd done and went over.

'I'm absolutely dying with hunger,' she said. 'I can't even remember when I last ate. Could you spare a famished friend a grain or two?'

'But surely last summer you put some food away to feed yourself this winter?' said an ant.

'Not at all,' said the cicada. 'I was far too busy singing for that kind of carry-on.'

'Well,' said the ant, who had a bit of a reputation as a wag and saw the chance here for a juicy quip at the cicada's expense, 'sing like a fool all summer, you'd better be prepared to dance the winter away.'

Where you cannot catch anything, it is useless to stretch out your hand.

3

SELF-DECEPTION, STUPIDITY AND IDIOCY

41.

The Desperate Vendor

A man in need of money carved a statue of Hermes and took it to the market to sell. Good wares sell themselves, or so he thought. Sadly, though he waited several hours, no buyer came near him.

'I'll need to do something here if I'm going to shift this,' he said to himself. He thought for a moment and then – inspiration.

'God for sale,' he shouted. 'He will give you whatever goods you want *and* profits – guaranteed. You demand, he delivers!'

'Well,' asked a passer-by, 'if he's so damned good what are you selling him for? Shouldn't you keep him for yourself?'

'I know,' said the vendor, 'I know I should keep him. But he's so slow and I need the money – now!'

The saving of a man is the holding of his tongue.

42.

The Copy-Cat

Spring. A flock of sheep in a field with their ram. An eagle swooped in, seized a lamb in its talons and carried it off.

A jackdaw sitting on the wall of the field saw this.

'My word,' he said. 'If an eagle can do that, why can't I? I'm just as good as him, aren't I? Of course I am. Well then, I shall do the same. But it won't be a lamb I take. Oh no. My prize will be something much bigger.'

The jackdaw climbed as high as he could into the sky. Then, with a great whirring of wings, he came shooting down

The Copy-Cat, part I

The Copy-Cat, part II

and landed on the fleecy back of the ram. He extended his claws then pulled them in and went to rise, expecting to carry the ram with him. But the ram was too heavy for him to lift.

His plan had foundered, the jackdaw realised, and now there was nothing for it but to let go and fly away. But when he tried to let go and fly upwards he found he couldn't. His claws were tangled in the ram's fleece. He flapped and writhed but nothing he did was enough to escape. He was trapped.

By and by the shepherd came to check his flock and saw the jackdaw attached to the ram's back. The shepherd went over.

'Thought you'd act the eagle, did you?' he said to the frantic jackdaw. 'You should know by now: be the master of your heart, but do not make it your master.'

He got the jackdaw free, clipped his wings, took him home and put him in a cage that hung over the fireplace. The shepherd's children gathered round and peered in through the bars at the prisoner with his clipped wings. He looked decidedly odd to them and they didn't know what to make of him.

'What sort of bird is that?' asked one.

'A jackdaw,' said the shepherd, 'but he wants to be taken for an eagle.'

The first stage of folly is to think oneself great.

43.

The Slave

A rich man bought an Ethiopian slave. The buyer had never seen black skin before, and he was certain the slave's previous owner must have refused the man access to water. This was the only explanation he could come up with.

'Hot water,' he ordered his cook when he got home with his new purchase.

In the bathhouse the rich man began to scrub the slave.

Nothing happened, of course – the slave's black skin stayed black because black was what it was – but, undeterred, the rich man went on scrubbing.

'Your actions are pointless,' said the slave, who had just grasped what was happening. 'My skin is black, just as yours is white. Nothing can change it …'

But the master wouldn't listen. He just carried on.

Belief is invariably simpler than investigation and so infinitely preferred.

44.
The Goatherd and the Goat

Evening. 'Come on,' the goatherd called to his herd. 'Time to come in.'

All his animals ambled over to him bar one laggard. The goatherd threw a stone to encourage her. It hit her left horn and snapped it off.

'Oh no, I'm in trouble,' said the goatherd.

He ran to his victim.

'Don't tell the master about this,' he said. 'Please …'

'Are you serious?' said the goat. 'A horn on one side, no horn on the other and you think he won't notice?'

If it won't work, it won't work.

45.
The Bunch of Grapes and the Fox

A hungry fox spotted a bunch of lovely dark grapes hanging from a vine trained over a tall olive tree.

'They'll do me nicely,' he said. 'They've got my name written all over them, so they have.'

The fox leapt upwards and snapped his jaw shut, expecting to feel the delicious sensation of the fruit caught fast in his mouth. To his surprise, however, all he felt was the judder of his upper and lower teeth crashing against one another without any fruit in between to cushion the blow. He fell back to earth.

'If at first you don't succeed,' he said, 'try, try and try again.'

He tried a few more times and then he stopped. This was never going to work. The bunch he was going for was just too high for him – and it was the lowest one.

He walked away, and as he went the fox muttered, 'I don't know what I was thinking. Those grapes, they're not even ripe.'

A lie becomes true when you believe it.

46.

The Monkey and the Fox Dispute Their Nobility

The monkey and the fox traipsed along the road. They were arguing as to who was the better born and to support his claim each rattled off his titles and inheritances. Neither, of course, paid the slightest bit of attention to what the other one said. Each just talked over the other. That was how they were.

The road they were on passed a wall on the other side of which was a graveyard filled with tombstones.

The monkey stopped, leant on the wall, looked over and sighed.

'What are you sighing for?' said the fox.

'Every single grave,' said the monkey, 'is the resting place of a great ancestor of mine. I stand today on the shoulders of those dead giants, you know.'

'Incredible,' said the fox, 'that we should just happen to walk past a graveyard filled with your forebears.'

'I know,' the monkey agreed.

'And with them all being dead, not a single one can stand up and call you a liar. How lucky is that?'

Liars boast most when there is no one to contradict them.

47.

Hermes and the Man Bitten by an Ant

Out at sea a storm, fierce, ferocious, terrifying …

In the harbour a crowd gathered to watch a ship labouring towards them. Hoping to help the vessel reach the safety of their harbour, they cheered her on. This did no good. The boat capsized, pitching its entire company into the water. The crowd gasped. Their collective opinion was that no mariner could survive in the furious sea, and therefore the ship's entire company should be counted as lost.

'There were good as well as bad men on board that ship,' said a man who was one of the crowd, watching. 'Yet the gods, who claim to be just, took them all, good and bad, which hardly seems fair.'

The speaker felt a sharp nip on his toe at that moment. He looked down and saw an ant-heap.

'Think you're safe?' he said, imagining the ant who had bitten him was hiding inside the ant-heap, listening. 'Well, think again.'

The man stamped on the heap killing all the ants inside.

By chance Hermes was nearby. He witnessed everything. He materialised in front of the fractious onlooker.

'You denounce the gods for letting the good and the bad perish together at sea,' said the god, 'yet when you get a nip from one ant, you exterminate his whole colony. You mightn't admit it, but you and the gods are no different. Know thyself.'

God protect us from him who has read but one book.

48.

The Stargazer

A cloudless, moonless night – perfect for stargazing.

The stargazer slipped through the city gate, went out into the fields beyond the walls and began to wander about, gazing up at the sky.

'I've never seen the stars as bright as they are tonight,' he said.

The stargazer felt himself pitching forward and then – bang! He was on his back, in pain, shocked, winded, disoriented.

The stargazer began to moan. He was heard by a passer-by.

'I'd better go and see who that is,' thought the passer-by.

He followed the noise. It led him to a dry well. He looked over its lip and saw the famous stargazer lying on his back at the bottom.

'If it isn't our famous stargazer,' the passer-by called down. 'Well, you know what they say. Every sheep is hung up by its own leg. I suppose you were so busy looking up at the sky you forgot to look where you were going?'

'And I suppose you're now going to tell me,' said the stargazer, 'that people like me who don't pay attention to what's right in front of them invariably come a cropper?'

'I was,' said the passer-by. 'How did you know?'

'It's written in the stars.'

'Really? Well, you learn something every day, don't you? Lucky me that I should be passing just now.'

'The man's an idiot,' thought the stargazer.

Every fool loves his cap.

49.

The Fox and the Frog Doctor

The frog hopped up on a stump in the marsh where he lived and shouted out to all the animals within earshot. 'I am a doctor – and not just any doctor. Oh no. I am the greatest doctor who has ever lived and there is no disease I cannot cure.'

At this moment a fox was passing. 'A doctor you say?' he called. 'What? Look at your rear legs, all bent and lame. Why should any animal believe you can cure them when you can't cure your own limp? Physician, heal thyself.'

Of course, the fox didn't know the legs of frogs were meant to be as they were.

Because there are fools other fools look wise.

50.

The File and the House-Ferret

In a small town, early in the evening, there was still light in the sky but in the houses the lamps were already burning and their tapers were throwing out a weak, yellowish light.

In an empty street a house-ferret crept along, hugging close to the buildings so she would not be seen. She came to a forge. She saw the blacksmith was gone and that he had left the door to his premises ajar.

'I've never been in the forge,' said the house-ferret. 'Well, open door, no blacksmith, now's my chance.'

The house-ferret crept in. The dark interior, lit only by the embers glowing in the hearth, smelled of burnt charcoal, scorch and hot metal. The house-ferret jumped up on to the workbench and found a file lying on its back, its rough side showing dimly in the quarter-light.

The File and the House-Ferret

'Smells horsy,' the ferret said, sniffing this, to her, mysterious object, for she'd never seen anything like this tool before. She was right, it did smell horsy, for the smith used it to file the hooves of the horses he shod.

The ferret ran her tongue up and down the face of the tool. The crosshatching scoured her skin away and she tasted blood, though she didn't know it was hers.

'Blood,' she thought. 'Meat!' She went on licking until, at last, her tongue was quite gone but her stomach was full.

The fool who falls into the fire rarely falls out of it.

51.

The Frozen Snake and the Ploughman

A deep winter's morning. The ground was hard and white.

The ploughman, on his way to feed his horses, spotted a snake rigid with cold under the water trough in the yard.

Without thinking, the ploughman picked up the frozen creature and slipped it under his shirt. The snake revived and bit his benefactor just below his left nipple. The venom was in his heart in an instant. The ploughman collapsed onto the icy cobbles. The snake slipped out from under his clothes and started to wriggle away.

'Why did I pick him up?' the ploughman wondered, 'when he was always going to bite?'

'We live less by reason than by instinct,' came the answer, his last thought before his mind went black.

You mightn't think it will happen but it will.

52.

The Children and Their Father, the Farmer

The farmer was dying. He summoned his children. 'I'll be gone soon,' he said, 'but worry not. You're provided for. I've hidden the answer to all your needs in my fields. You just have to find it.'

Once he was dead, his children, assuming he had meant buried treasure, hoed every inch of his land. They found nothing. However, they turned the ground so well as they searched that their father's vines flourished.

Over the following years it was the same story. The farmer's children hoed and hoed as they searched for the treasure that wasn't there and the ground, responding to their work, supported the vines and the vines produced magnificent fruit.

Misunderstandings aren't always bad.

53.

The Servants and Their Mistress

A lonely farm, a winter's morning. On the hen-house roof the cockerel saw the first glimmer of dawn and crowed; this woke the old woman in her cold bedroom in the farmhouse. She lit a candle, pulled on her dressing gown and climbed the rickety stairs to the attic. Under the low sloping eaves she found her servant girls sleeping in their narrow cots, their breathing slow and steady.

'Mr Cockerel bids you rise,' she called. She clapped her hands and stamped on the bare wooden floorboards. 'Time to get up, girls. Time for work. Come on, I want you all out of your beds ...'

The servants pushed their covers back and got up.

'Good girls,' said the mistress. 'See you all in the kitchen shortly. I hope you're ready to work.'

The mistress went back down the rickety stairs to dress.

In the attic, the servant girls set about getting ready, some washing their faces in cold water, others combing their hair, others again pulling on their icy work dresses and aprons.

'Wouldn't you love to lie on?' said one.

'Oh, I wish,' said another. 'I'm exhausted.' She was. They all were. The mistress worked them without let-up.

'You know,' said a third servant girl, 'if the cockerel didn't wake her, then she wouldn't wake us, would she?'

'In which case,' said a fourth, 'we know what to do, don't we?'

That afternoon, while their mistress was sleeping by the

fire in the kitchen, the servant girls cornered the cockerel in the farmyard. The first grabbed one wing, the second the other wing, the third the legs and the fourth, who had the big kitchen knife, grabbed his head and sliced through his neck. The other three released the headless body and it stood up and tottered a couple of steps, red, warm blood spurting from its neck, before collapsing on the ground. The servant girls dropped the cockerel's body and head into a sack they had also brought. They hurried with the sack to the dung-heap and buried it deep in the mire.

The next morning, not long after the first glimmerings of dawn showed, the old woman woke with a start. The silence was unnerving. 'Where's my cockerel?' she murmured in the darkness. 'Why hasn't he crowed?'

She went up to the attic where she found her servant girls sleeping in their narrow cots.

'Time to get up, girls. Time for work,' she called.

She clapped her hands and stamped on the bare wooden floorboards. 'My cockerel never crowed,' she said. 'Can you believe it? For years, every morning he's woken me faithfully but this morning – nothing.'

She went down to the ground floor and out into the yard. She looked at the roof ridge where the cockerel would normally have stood but he wasn't there.

'He can't have vanished into thin air,' she said. 'Where's he gone?'

That night the old woman's sleep was fitful because she knew she wouldn't be woken as usual; she woke in darkness long before dawn.

'Now my cockerel's gone,' she said, 'how do I know it's time to rise? I don't, so I'll just assume it's now!'

And from then on, with no cockerel to wake her, she woke earlier, and so in turn she woke her servants earlier, which meant their lives were worse than before the cockerel vanished.

The birch one makes for oneself hits the hardest.

54.

The Lion and the Stag at the Spring

The stag came to drink at the spring and, bending down, he saw a wavering image of himself looking back at him.

'Those antlers of mine,' he said, 'they're superb! But my legs, so thin, so spindly, so ridiculous.'

The stag was so lost in his thoughts he didn't hear the lion creeping towards him until the beast roared and leapt.

The stag, shaken from his reverie, jumped sideways before the lion got him. He began to run. The lion followed. The ground they raced across was open; the stag pulled ahead and increased the distance between himself and the lion. But then, why wouldn't he? The stag was a creature in his prime, a glory.

Trees loomed ahead, the edge of the forest. There was nowhere for the stag to run except in. And he did. Now – calamity. His enormous antlers became entangled in a tree's dense lower branches and he couldn't free himself. He was caught.

'Pride and real value never can agree,' he shouted. 'I hated my legs, yet they did their best to save me, while I loved my antlers that are my undoing.'

These were the stag's last words.

A moment later the lion had savaged his neck, his blood gushed and he was dead.

What is worth most is usually valued least.

55.

The Breakdown of the Chariot of Hermes

The great god Zeus summoned the lesser god Hermes.

'I want you to load your chariot with lies, villainy and

fraud,' said Zeus, 'and go down to earth and distribute the stuff round everyone.'

Hermes nodded.

'Now remember,' Zeus continued, 'every nation gets the same amount. We can't have any one race better at lying, villainy and fraud than any other, can we? It wouldn't be fair.'

Hermes loaded his chariot, drove it to earth and set about disbursing an equal amount of his cargo around the population of every country he passed through. Then – disaster. The wheel came off his chariot. He couldn't move. He was stuck and the inhabitants of this country where he'd broken down, thinking his cargo must be precious, stole it all during the night while he was sleeping.

The consequences of the theft were two-fold: one, Hermes had to abandon his task and return to Olympus, and two, the inhabitants of the country who'd stolen his cargo acquired a reputation for being not only the greatest liars, villains and fraudsters on earth, but a race so bad they didn't even have the word for 'truth' in their language.

All over the world, nations tell this same story about their neighbours.

56.

The Two Enemies in the One Boat

Two men who hated one another happened to find themselves on the same boat. To ensure they wouldn't meet and fight, one put himself in the prow and the other in the stern.

A storm rose. Seawater poured over the sides faster than the sailors could bail out the vessel. She began to sink.

'Helmsman,' shouted the man in the stern, 'which part will go down first?'

'The prow, of course,' said the helmsman. 'Does it matter?'

'Yes, it does,' said the man, 'because knowing I'll see my enemy die first, I now know I'll die happy.'

A man will take anything so long as his enemy's hurt first.

57.

The Jar of Things That Did People Good

The things that did people good lived on Olympus with the gods. One day Zeus summoned them all and put them in a jar. Then he hammered a cork bung into the jar's neck and sealed it with hot, black pitch.

'Hermes,' he shouted.

The lesser god appeared.

'You'll take this to earth and leave it in the care of a certain man; I'll give you his name in a moment. You'll tell him never to open it.'

'This is not a good idea,' thought Hermes, but he said nothing.

As instructed, the lesser god took the jar to earth and gave it to the man along with Zeus's instructions.

The man, being a man, was curious to know what was inside. Of course he was. He was a human being. One day he smashed the brittle pitch and levered the cork away. The things that did people good swarmed out of the jar's mouth.

'Where are we?' one of the small, light, gossamer, golden things asked the man.

'Earth,' said their liberator. 'Who are you?'

'The things that do people good.'

'Well, you've never been needed more than now,' he said. 'Life here is so hard, you know.'

'You can forget that,' said the one who'd spoken already. 'We're not staying in this repulsive place, are we?'

'Never,' the rest chorused.

And with that the things that do people good streamed back to Olympus and the gods.

'I shouldn't have let them out,' said the man. 'On the other hand, if I hadn't I wouldn't have acquired this excellent jar, and if the gods smile I should have plenty of wine to put in it later this year.'

Hope is the physician of each misery.

58.

The Reflection and the Dog

A summer's afternoon, late on. A dog, a piece of meat in its mouth, approached the footbridge – three stout planks lashed together, lying just a hand's breadth above the stream.

His paws – first the front ones, then the back ones – went onto the boards. They were stout and thick and smooth from wear. In the stream just below, a frog swam along, kicking his green legs behind.

'What's this?' said the dog. He was seeing something out of the corner of his eye. He looked down at the stream's surface. Another dog, was it? It was. And what's more, another dog with a piece of meat in its mouth. How lucky was this? He already had a piece of meat and now another dog with a second piece had appeared right in front of him. If he took that piece then he would have two pieces, and two pieces were better than one.

He let go what he had in his mouth and lunged forward. To his surprise he found his head under water. He lifted his head out and realised, for he saw it bobbing on the surface, that his piece of meat, when he had let it go, had fallen into the stream. He went to retrieve it but too late. His meat was carried under the bridge. He moved to the far side, thinking to catch it when it appeared, but by the time he had got over

The Reflection and the Dog

his meat was already floating away down the stream and out of his reach.

As the dog watched his piece getting smaller, he realised he was not alone, for the dog from before, no meat in his mouth now either and an unhappy expression on his face, was looking back up at him from the stream.

'I had meat, wanted more, lost everything,' he said. 'It's true what they say: he who takes what he does not need ends with nothing …'

As he spoke, the other dog seemed to be saying exactly the same thing as he was saying, word for word. For a second he thought it strange, but then he decided no, they were in the same situation so they were bound to say the same thing.

The dog turned and padded on across the footbridge, and as he did he wondered why he hadn't seen the other's piece of meat floating away. Odd that.

Charity gives itself rich: covetousness hoards itself poor.

59.

The Ass and His Burdens

The ass made his way along the stony path. His driver followed, prodding him with a stick as they went and calling, 'Go on.'

The ass's panniers were crammed with salt. The driver had already pre-sold the salt in the village where he lived. Once he got home a fat fee awaited him.

'Go on,' the driver shouted again in his wheedling voice.

'Go on?' thought the ass. 'Why does the idiot keep repeating the same stupid phrase? What else would I be doing but going on? Oh, I hate this man.'

They came to a ford across a fast-flowing river. The ass went forward, heading for the far bank. The stones under his hooves were uneven and next thing he was no longer in touch with the solid floor of the riverbed and he was tumbling and then he was sinking and now he was right under the water, even his head was under the water, and then he felt his bridle being yanked and his hooves went down and he felt the bed again under his hooves and he stood up.

And what's this? He didn't feel so heavy.

'You stupid, stupid animal,' he heard his driver shouting. 'The salt's all melted in the water and now it's all gone, you stupid beast.'

A blow on his scrawny rump and then another on his ear.

'The whole load lost,' said the driver, 'ruined. Now I'll have to buy a second load to take home and that's it – that's my profit wiped out. That's me ruined, and all because my stupid ass couldn't keep his footing crossing a ford.'

More blows, more shouting. The beating was vicious. On the other hand, not to have the heavy load weighing down on his narrow, bowed back, this was wonderful ...

Another day. The same ass, though this time he was loaded with sponges his driver had bought from a fisherman and was taking to the city to sell. Sponges are light but the load was enormous and the going was hard as he moved along, the driver shouting, 'Go on,' and prodding him with his stick as usual.

The ass reached the edge of a wide, shallow river. The ass remembered the time he'd tumbled with the salt and how wonderfully light he had been when he stood back up. 'Why don't I repeat the trick?' he thought. 'And that way I'll get rid of this load.'

He threw himself into the water.

'You idiot, you stupid, stupid idiot ...'

Kicks and shouts and his bridle being yanked. The ass paused to let the water do its lightening work, then he put out his hooves and found the riverbed. He would enjoy the next moment, standing slowly, feeling the weight gone from his poor bowed back.

'My driver can beat me as much as he wants,' the ass said to himself. 'I will be light and I can take it.'

He pressed his hooves down on the river bed. But what was this? Bearing down on him, the most incredible weight.

He couldn't stand. What? Try again. No. The weight. The weight was incredible. He was not any lighter. On the contrary, he was far heavier than when he'd gone into the water in the first place. What was happening? He couldn't stand. He couldn't get himself back up on his feet.

'You idiot,' his driver shouted. 'The sponges are full of water … I'll have to dry them in the sun and that'll take all day. I'll miss the market. Stupid, stupid ass …'

Disaster only enters the door that one has left open for it.

60.

The Passengers at Sea

A ship rolling on a roiling, stormy sea. At the back, by the helmsman, passengers cowering in terror.

'Will we live?' one shouted at him.

'Who knows,' the helmsman shouted back. 'It's in the lap of the gods.'

'Oh dear god, Poseidon,' the passengers cried. 'Let us live. Let us make it safely to harbour. Let us see our loved ones again. Let us kiss their beloved faces and hold their soft hands and hear their sweet voices …'

Did the god hear? It is not recorded; but what is known is that shortly after this the sea began to quieten, the waves to flatten and the wind to drop, while the sky above went from black to grey and then, miracle of miracles, the clouds parted and watery patches of blue showed here and there.

The passengers wrung the salt water from their clothes and wiped away the salt from their faces.

'Yes,' said one, 'the worst is behind us. We are going to live.'

These words had an extraordinary effect on every passenger. They would not drown and be washed ashore,

The Passengers at Sea

they realised, bloated, bruised and eyeless. No. They would make it safely to harbour. They would see their loved ones. They would live.

'We are going to live!' the passengers cried. A woman began to dance, and before long every passenger was stamping, laughing, clapping, singing and dancing.

'Hang on,' shouted the helmsman. 'You think that's it? Dream on, citizens. There will be more storms ahead. You do know that, don't you?'

But none of the passengers replied. They just went on roistering.

He does not hear what he does not like.

4

AMBITION, OVERWEENING AND OVERREACH

61.

The Debtor from Athens

A man borrowed heavily from a moneylender. The date the money was due to be repaid came and went. The lender summoned the debtor to his counting house.

'I don't care how you do it,' said the moneylender, 'but you get my money to me by the end of the day or you go to jail.'

The debtor fetched the last thing he owned – a sow – and brought her back to the street where lender's counting house was.

'Sow for sale,' the debtor shouted. 'Miracle sow.'

'How so?' asked a passer-by.

'Say the word "boar" to her,' said the debtor, 'you get boars. But say "sow", you get sows, as many as you need.'

The moneylender sitting at his counting table inside heard everything the debtor said and he went out to him.

'And if I say "billy-goats" I get billies?' he said. 'And if I say "nannies" I get nanny-goats?'

The debtor nodded.

'So it really is true,' said the moneylender. 'In the field of dreams hopes grow like weeds.'

A debtor always lies.

62.

The Eagle and the Two Cocks

Two cockerels fought as to which of them would be master over a flock of hens. When the fight was over the loser melted

The Eagle and the Two Cocks

away and hid in a thicket while the victor hopped onto a wall and crowed, 'I won, I won.'

Floating high in the sky overhead, an eagle saw the victor on the wall below, his head tilted back as he proclaimed his triumph.

'Ah,' said the eagle, 'the proud always punishes himself, doesn't he?'

He dropped from the sky, seized the victorious cockerel and carried him off, squawking and squealing.

The loser emerged from the thicket. He did not hop up on the wall and proclaim his victory. He just went to the hens. He was number one now.

Pride is the clearest hallmark of stupidity.

63.

The Foxes on the Bank of the River

The foxes' favourite drinking place on the river was a spit that jutted from the bank from which it was easy and safe to lean down. One evening, however, when they arrived, they found the spit washed away and a whirlpool where it had been.

'It's too risky to drink here,' said a cautious old fox with a mantle of white on his chin. 'We'll find somewhere else.'

'Don't be ridiculous,' said a young fox, who believed he was the bravest of them all. 'This is perfectly safe.'

He jumped into the whirlpool, imagining he would drink his fill while he was spun about and then scramble out. But the water swirled him about so fiercely it was all he could do to keep from being sucked under.

'How is it?' the other foxes shouted looking down, half-appalled, half-amazed.

'Gorgeous,' the young fox shouted back. A moment after, the whirlpool ejected him into the river and he was borne away downstream.

'Don't abandon us,' his fellow foxes shouted. 'We need you to show us where to drink.'

'Sorry, can't help you now,' the young fox shouted back. 'Got a message to deliver. I'll show you later, when I'm back.'

The river carried him round a bend and out of sight. The other foxes never saw him again.

Even the fortune teller does not know his own destiny.

64.

The Greedy Fox

The fox smelled food that some shepherds had left in a hollow inside an ancient oak tree. He looked through the hole in the trunk and saw a plump loaf and a thick salami inside. The hollow was doubling as some shepherd's larder, he realised.

The fox wriggled through the hole and got into the dark, woody, musty interior. He ate everything the shepherd had left there.

'That was delicious,' he said.

He put his nose through the hole he'd come in by and began to wriggle back the other way. He got his head out. He got his chest and front paws out. Then – catastrophe. His stomach was so swollen it wouldn't go through, and since his stomach wouldn't go through, the fox couldn't get out.

'Oh no,' the fox moaned. 'What shall I do?'

Another fox happened to be passing at this point. This second fox heard the moans of the prisoner and stopped.

'What is it?' asked the passer-by. 'What's wrong?'

'It's like this,' said the fox who was stuck. 'I spotted a shepherd's lunch in here, so I climbed in and ate it. Now my stomach's so expanded I can't get out. I'm stuck.'

'Oh, don't worry,' said the passer-by. 'A few hours and you'll shrink back to what you were and then you'll be able to get out.'

'I suppose,' said the fox who was trapped.

He lay down on the floor and went to sleep. While he was sleeping his stomach would shrink and then when he woke he would be able to get out? Wasn't that what he'd been told?

The fox was woken by a human voice.

'You've eaten my food, you wretch.' It was the shepherd whose food he'd eaten shouting in at him.

'I'm sorry,' said the fox, 'I shouldn't –'

The shepherd went away and came back. 'Others' bread will always cost dearly,' he shouted. 'See how you like this.'

He stuffed something in through the hole and it landed by the fox. Though it was dark inside the hollow, the fox could just make out that it was a cloth bag. 'More food?' wondered the fox. 'Surely not?'

The bag began to move. Something was inside. There was a low, ominous hiss. The head of a snake nosed forward out of the bag's mouth …

The shepherd, his face close to the hole, was watching and laughing.

Rather too little than too much.

65.

The Python and the Fox

Afternoon. A fig tree heavy with lovely purple-skinned fruit and, stretched out below, a python, sleeping.

A fox meandered past. He saw the serpent, stopped.

'Oh,' said the fox. He was impressed. 'I have a reputation,' the fox said, speaking in a hushed voice so as not to wake the python. 'I am known as clever, resourceful and cunning. But what are they in comparison to size? I must be, I will be, as big as this creature, or I am nothing.'

He lay down beside the python and stretched and stretched and stretched … until the skin covering his belly ripped open.

In the evening, when he woke, the python was very surprised to see the fox lying dead beside him, with his belly split and his guts tumbled out.

'What a happy coincidence,' said the python, 'that I should fall asleep here and wake to find this.'

He opened his jaw and by the time night came the fox was gone, swallowed whole.

Don't compete out of your category.

66.

The Man and the False Promise

A man lay dying in bed, his wife and doctor beside him.

'There's no hope for me, doctor, is there?' he said.

'None whatsoever,' said the doctor.

'Oh ye gods,' the man called out. 'Let me live and I promise I'll sacrifice a hundred oxen in your honour.'

'What are you saying?' said the poor man's wife, who knew he couldn't afford one ox let alone a hundred. 'You're a poor man. How do you propose to pay for these?'

'Oh, I don't,' said the man. 'If I recover I've got no intention of spending the rest of my life in hock to the gods. That'd be mad ...'

It is best to tell lies alone.

67.

The Chancer

Evening, a tavern, a party of drinkers, the chancer among them ...

'Dear friends,' he said. 'I say the Oracle at Delphi is a

fraud and, what's more, I can prove it. Now, who'll bet I can't?'

His fellow drinkers were surprised. They knew the chancer said provocative things and liked to make improbable bets but this was different: this was the Oracle at Delphi he was talking about and the oracle was infallible.

'How are you going to prove the oracle's a fraud?' several asked. They all pressed him to answer but he wouldn't say how he'd prove it, only that he could. His friends were by turns baffled and curious, and though not all of them were convinced, by the end of the night several had agreed to bet against him.

The next day the chancer went to the oracle's temple wearing a long cloak, a sparrow in his hand hidden underneath. The chancer joined the line of supplicants waiting their turn to put their question to the oracle who lived behind a cleft in the rock on which the temple was built …

Time passed. The chancer got to the top of the queue. He bent towards the cleft. He felt the sparrow pulsing between his fingers. His plan, now, was to say to the oracle, 'Is what I hold in my hand lifeless or living?'

If the oracle said, 'Lifeless,' he intended to release the sparrow and let it fly around the temple. This would prove the oracle wrong. And if the oracle said, 'Living,' he intended to strangle the sparrow and produce the body. Again, this would prove the oracle wrong. So, either way, whatever answer was given, he would expose the oracle as a fraud. Or so he thought.

'Oracle,' said the chancer, 'is what I hold in my hand lifeless or living?'

'That's a trick question,' said the oracle, speaking through the cleft in a loud, clear, resolute voice, 'because, of course, it depends on what you do to the bird you hold in your hand, hidden under your cloak. Are you going to kill it or are you going to let it live? You tell me which you've done, and then I'll tell you whether it's lifeless or living.'

Who thinks to deceive has already deceived himself.

68.

The Blowhard

The blowhard was a talented athlete but also prickly, argumentative and bitter. Nobody much liked him in his city, so he left and went abroad ...

He returned some years later and, on his first day back, in the main square, he bumped into a group of sportsmen he'd known when he was younger.

'I've done rather well for myself in foreign parts,' he said, 'much better than if I'd stayed here. I did a long jump in Rhodes, for instance, which has yet to be equalled by an Olympic champion. If any of you ever visit that remarkable city, just mention my name and anyone will tell you about my incredible leap, the longest ever made there.'

'We don't need to go there to do that,' one of those listening said. 'Rhodes is right here. The sight is more truthful than the voice. Go on, make the jump now.'

Deed shows proof.

69.

The Fox and the Farmer

One night, a fox went to a farm and killed every bird in the hen-house. When the farmer came out in the morning and saw the carnage, he was incensed.

'Mr Fox,' he vowed, 'I'll pay you back for what you've done.'

He set a trap and caught the fox, alive.

'Right,' said the farmer, 'I promised I would pay you back, and I'm a man of my word.'

He tied a rope soaked in oil to the fox's tail. Then he set the rope alight and released the fox on the track in front of his farmhouse. The fox ran about trailing the burning rope, yelping and screaming as the flames spread up his tail.

'Hey, stupid, your tail's on fire,' the farmer shouted. It was great sport watching the fox running about in a frenzy trying to escape the flames it could never escape. But then, crazed and panic-stricken, the fox left the track and bolted towards the field where the farmer's wheat crop, tall and lovely and dry, stood ready and waiting to be harvested.

'Hey, no, not that way,' the farmer bellowed.

The farmer ran his fastest but his fastest wasn't fast enough to catch the fox before it got right into the middle of the field and set the crop alight.

The flames spread and the whole field became a burning, raging conflagration. The farmer stood on the edge and watched. He felt the heat of the flames on his face and smelled the familiar smell of burning straw. It made his eyes sting and his throat hurt.

'What will my children eat if we have no bread?' he said.

But there was no one there to hear him, let alone answer.

Do not lift the club too high, it may fall on your head.

70.

The Statue and the Man

A poor man owned a wooden statue of a god.

One day, when he had nothing to eat, as he had done many times before, he prostrated himself before the statue. 'Dear powerful one,' he beseeched, 'grant me food.'

But nothing happened. No food appeared.

'Year after year I implore you to help,' the poor man continued, for he was filled with anger now, 'and year after year you do nothing. Well, I've had my bellyful of you and your so-called help. I don't want you anymore. You're useless.'

He picked the figure up by the legs and smashed the head against the wall. The wood split and gold coins poured out.

'What a queer, contradictory, inconsistent god you are,' the poor man said. 'I honour you for years – nothing. I bash your head in – you shower me with gold.'

Men are the pack of cards of the gods.

71.

Herakles and the Ox-Driver

Winter, a bad road, a wooden cart pulled by two bony oxen. The going was hard. At the bottom of a hill, under the weight of its load, the cart sank into the mud and stopped.

The carter was on the verge alongside the cart. 'Come on,' he shouted at the oxen. 'Pull ...'

The oxen strained but they could not shift the cart.

'Herakles, we're stuck,' said the carter. He admired the god and he believed Herakles knew this. 'You call yourself strong. Well, now's your chance to prove it.'

The god, who just happened by chance to be in the vicinity, appeared before the carter.

'I don't see you making much of an effort,' he said. 'I don't see you with your shoulder at the wheel, trying to push the cart out of the mud. You're just standing around demanding your oxen pull harder or that I come and help. By this stage in your life you should know that heaven helps those who help themselves, but given you haven't, you can forget about help from me or any other quarter.'

With that, the god vanished, feeling pretty pleased with himself and his pretty speech. Nothing really beat putting people, stupid people, in their place.

It is an iron law of the universe that the importunate never prosper.

72.

Chance and the Ploughman

The ploughman was ploughing. He steered his plough and its blade cut through the dark, moist soil, leaving a neat furrow behind. Then the plough bucked and there was a clunk, the sound of the cutting edge striking a hidden obstruction.

The ploughman heaved on his reins. 'Whoa!'

The horse halted.

'Whatever that was,' the ploughman said, 'I'll have to dig it out in case it breaks the blade next time.'

He scrabbled and rummaged in the earth with his hands until he located what the plough had struck.

'What have we here?' the ploughman said.

It didn't feel like a stone, which surprised him. It felt long, jagged and metallic. He closed his fingers tight around it and pulled. Once he had it clear of the earth, what he found he was holding was a crown of gold.

'A gift from Mother Earth,' he shouted. 'Well, goddess, I thank you.'

He carried his find home and, since he believed this was her gift, he set the crown on the head of the bust of Mother Earth that he kept on his mantelpiece.

That night the Goddess of Chance spoke to the ploughman in his dreams: 'Why do you honour Mother Earth?' she said. 'It was I who wanted you to be rich; it was I who gave you the crown. Not her. As should be obvious to you.'

'Why so?' said the ploughman.

'Just think about it,' said the goddess. 'Supposing you lost the crown, or it was stolen, who would you blame? Her? Mother Earth? No. It would be me, Chance! That's who. I'm the one who sources these gifts, just as I'm the one who makes them vanish. You should know better.'

When you drink the water, forget the cup, think of the spring.

The Sculptor and Hermes

73.

Diogenes at the River

Diogenes was travelling on foot. He came to the bank of a fast-flowing river.

'How am I going to get across?' he asked, perplexed.

A local man, who knew the river, was standing nearby. He heard Diogenes.

'I'll carry you over,' said the man. 'Jump up.'

Diogenes got onto his back and the man carried him across and set him down.

'My purse is empty,' said the philosopher, 'and I've nothing to give you except thanks, which are no good to anyone.'

'Don't worry, you owe me nothing,' said the man. 'Just to be of service, that's payment enough for me.'

At that moment another traveller appeared beside them and said, staring at the fast-flowing river, 'How am I going to get across?' – exactly as Diogenes had done a few minutes earlier.

'I'll carry you over,' said the local man. 'Jump up on my back.'

The stranger leapt up on the man's back and, his legs secured, the local stepped down and began to splash across.

'Well, now I've seen it all,' Diogenes shouted after the pair. 'It wasn't kindness that made you carry me over. No. It was mania, wasn't it? You simply can't stop yourself carrying travellers backwards and forwards, can you?'

Happily, the roar of the river drowned out the philosopher's words.

Who doesn't want to be thought special?

74.

The Sculptor and Hermes

The lesser god Hermes wanted to know what men thought of him. Highly, he hoped. So he travelled to earth, disguised himself as a mortal and walked into a sculptor's studio filled with statues finished and ready for sale.

'Can I help you?' said the sculptor.

'That one,' said Hermes pointing at a huge marble representation of Zeus. How much?'

The sculptor named a price, which was quite a lot less than Hermes had expected.

'And that one?' Hermes waved at a statue of Juno, Zeus's wife.

'Oh, she's more,' said the sculptor, 'much more.'

'And this one?' Hermes waved at a statue of himself.

'Ah, him, Zeus's messenger,' said the sculptor, 'and bearer of bad news.'

'And, let's not forget,' said Hermes, 'the god of profit as well. I suppose he's rather expensive.'

'Not at all,' said the sculptor. 'If you take the first two, I'll throw him in for free.'

By your deeds shall you be known.

75.

Teiresias and Hermes

Hermes, inclined by temperament to doubt everything, liked nothing better than to have his doubts confirmed.

'They say the blind prophet from Thebes, Teiresias, is able to divine the truth from watching wild birds,' he said one day. 'Well, I'll show the world they're deceived.'

The god disguised himself as a mortal, travelled to earth,

then stole and hid all Teiresias's cattle. Then he went to Teiresias to set his scheme to unmask the seer in motion.

'Teiresias,' said Hermes, 'all your cattle have gone, you know. They've vanished. I bet the birds didn't tell you that was coming.'

This was the first Teiresias knew about his herd's disappearance. He hadn't been forewarned. 'No,' Teiresias agreed, 'they didn't.'

'And are you going to get your cattle back?'

'Oh yes, don't worry, I'll find the thief,' said Teiresias. 'Come with me. You can be my eyes.'

Teiresias took Hermes to the edge of Thebes to observe the birds and, thanks to them, to divine who the thief was.

'What bird do you see now in the sky?' Teiresias asked.

'An eagle,' said Hermes, as he watched one flying left to right across the sky.

'No, that's no help to this case,' said Teiresias. 'Can you see anything else?'

'I can see a sea-crow on a tree,' said Hermes.

'What's he doing?' asked Teiresias.

'He's raising his eyes heavenwards ... now he's stretching his head towards the sun ... and now he's calling ... can you hear?'

'Yes,' said the blind seer, 'I hear his cry. And now, let me tell you what the sea-crow said. He's just sworn only you, Hermes, can return my cattle. No one else can. So may I have them back?'

He who digs a grave is first to fall into it.

76.

The Kite and the Snake

The kite cruised through the warm, still air. Below the bird, the earth unfurled – trees, hedges, walls, meadows, streams.

In the midst of the serene landscape some small something moved.

'What's that?' asked the kite, dropping down.

'It's a little snake,' said the kite, now close enough to see. 'I'll come down behind. It won't know I'm coming. Then I'll have it.'

The kite swooped, hovered just above the snake, grasped his dry, slender body around the middle in his talons and rose. The snake was momentarily bewildered. He had been on the ground wriggling along and suddenly there was the ground below him and it was receding as he rose into the air. Now the snake twisted his head to look up and saw, just overhead, the belly of the kite, with his coat of feathers. The snake judged he had sufficient reach. He snapped his head up, burrowed through the feathers, bit through the kite's skin with his sharp front teeth and released his venom.

A shriek above and the kite's outstretched wings stopping suddenly and an instant of stillness between rising and falling.

Then the talons opened and down they went, side by side, kite and snake. They landed in long grass by the edge of a stream.

The snake, winded but alive, peered at the kite, his head at a strange angle, his beak slightly apart, his eyes wide.

'You bit me,' said the kite.

'When misfortune is asleep do not wake her,' said the snake. 'I never did you harm yet you took me from the ground and carried me into the sky intending to do me harm. You woke misfortune and she bit you. What else would she do?'

This was the last thing the kite heard.

Nothing has dared so much as ignorance.

77.

The Heron and the Wolf

The wolf had a nasty, jagged piece of bone stuck in his throat. He retched, he swallowed, he coughed, he gasped and he spat, but nothing that he did would get it out.

'I'll have to get someone to lean in and pluck it out,' said the wolf hoarsely, 'and there's only one creature that I know of who could perform such a task.'

He took himself to the lake and searched out the heron. He found the bird sitting in a low tree, an elongated creature with grey feathers and a marvellous long beak.

'I've something stuck in my throat,' said the wolf.

'Indeed,' said the heron. 'I hope you haven't come to me to complain.'

'No, I've come to ask your help.'

The wolf offered his terms. If the heron would pull the piece of bone out of his throat, the wolf would pay handsomely. He named a figure, a huge figure.

'I'm going to be rich, I'm going to be rich …' the heron said to himself. He was so excited at the thought of his fee, but he knew he had to keep his feelings hidden.

'Your terms are acceptable,' said the heron coolly.

'Get on with it then,' muttered the wolf. 'I'm in agony.'

The heron flew down from his perch and landed in front of the wolf.

'Open wide,' said the heron.

The wolf opened his mouth and the heron lent in. The wolf's teeth were yellow and dangerous, his tongue long and wet, and his breath moist and nauseating. The heron peered forward. At the back of the mouth, where the throat started, he saw it, caught fast in a fold of dark slippery flesh – the brown bone piece.

'Don't move, hold still, absolutely still,' said the heron.

He tilted his head and down and in went his long beak, over the wolf's tongue and all the way to the back, to the trapped bone fragment. The heron opened his beak just enough, pinched the bone piece hard with the beak ends and slowly reversed, pulling his beak and his head backwards. The bone piece slid out, and a spurt of blood spurted after it, for where it had lodged it had cut into the flesh. The heron jerked his head back. He was clear of the wolf's mouth. He dropped the bone piece on the grass.

'Done,' he said. 'Success.'

The wolf shook his head and swallowed and ran in a little circle, happy and joyful.

'It's out, it's out,' he cried.

He stopped and looked at the bone piece.

'It mightn't look like much,' said the wolf, 'but that small, nasty piece of bone has caused me so much misery.'

'Well, maybe that'll teach you not to eat so quickly,' said the heron.

'Whatever.' The wolf shook himself, turned and began to walk away.

'Excuse me,' said the heron. 'You can't leave yet. You haven't paid …'

The wolf stopped, turned. 'Pay you?' he said. 'Listen, mate, you've got your head safely in and out of my mouth without getting it bitten off. That's it. That's your payment. Now you go and tell all your friends about it. I'm sure they'll be impressed.'

The wolf walked away. The heron went back to his perch and stared down at the lake. Its surface was still, smooth and silvered.

The ingratitude of the bad is better than their attention.

78.

Spring and Winter

The world had turned from winter to spring, longer days, warmer days ...

'Well, would you look at everyone?' said Winter to Spring. 'They're swarming all over the countryside gathering flowers to stick in their hair and piling into boats and putting out to sea to go to foreign parts to meet friends. Now winter is passed they no longer need to be fearful of tempests and winds and atrocious weather. But it won't be for long. I'll be back soon enough and when I am, I will have my say. "Don't look up at the sky, the sun is gone," I'll say. "Look down at the earth on which you tread and to which you cling. My friends, winter is back and I'm in charge once again and that means one thing: your place is not out in the world but at home, behind shuttered windows and bolted doors, so get there ... " You'd think they'd have learnt that by now, wouldn't you? You'd think they'd know that. But look at them, they've forgotten, they've forgotten everything.'

'You don't understand, do you?' said Spring. 'They don't want you or like you and they are never happier than when they are rid of you. Me, on the other hand, who loves them, they love in return. When I am gone they think of nothing but my coming back and when I appear, look at them – they're full of joy. With you it's the other way round. You mean misery, so when you're gone they forget about you completely.'

Only he that loves is remembered by all.

79.

The Eagle and the Tortoise

'Teach me to fly,' said the tortoise to the eagle.

'Impossible,' said the eagle. 'You are not made for flight.

You have no wings. I can't teach you because you will never, ever manage it. Get it? You're earth bound.'

'But I know I can fly,' the tortoise said, 'if you will only teach me. And besides, I am entitled, by virtue of my age and my intelligence, to become a creature of the air like you.'

The tortoise pressed the point for hours. The eagle grew tired, irritated and finally annoyed.

'Right,' said the eagle. 'I'll teach you.'

The eagle closed his talons around the tortoise's back right leg and flew up into the sky. The dangling tortoise staring down saw the ground beneath receding as he was carried upwards.

They reached the clouds.

'Flying is simple,' said the eagle. 'You just flap those legs. Got it?'

'Got it,' said the tortoise.

The eagle uncurled his talons and released the tortoise. The tortoise paddled his feet. Nothing happened, only falling. 'I can't fly,' he said. 'I'm falling.'

His body turned and he was on his back looking up at the eagle and the clouds above receding as he dropped. His terror was terrible but on the edge of his thoughts the notion crossed his mind that either he was falling very slowly or he was very high for he had plenty of time as he went down to look above himself and wonder what was going to happen next, although it was a foregone conclusion …

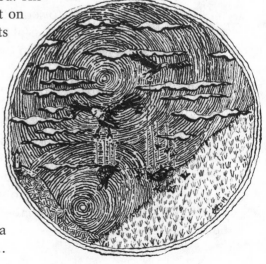

He smashed into a rock. His shell splintered. His tender insides were smeared about. Death was instant, which was fortunate, as this spared the tortoise the torment of living with the memory that his dying had only one architect – himself.

He who aims at an iron target gets the bullet in his face.

80.

The Hare and the Tortoise

'I am fastest out of us two,' said the tortoise.

'Don't say things like that,' said the hare. 'They only make you look stupid.'

'But I am,' the tortoise persisted.

'You're not,' said the hare, who was becoming mildly vexed. 'I am. Ask any animal who's the fastest out of you and me and you will get the same answer every time. Me. The hare. I. Am. The. Fastest.'

The tortoise would not concede this point. The hare began to resent his truculence.

'There's only one way to settle this,' said the hare. 'We will race from here, across the plains and all the way to the top of that distant mountain and that will settle this forever.'

The two set off. The hare sped far ahead. Then he stopped and looked back. Nothing. No sign of the tortoise anywhere on the bare plain that stretched behind.

'I can afford a snooze,' the hare thought. 'He's the slowest animal on earth, not to mention the most annoying. Look at him, ridiculous legs and that heavy shell he has to cart around. No, no, I've nothing to worry about. I can take a nice long nap and I'll still be across the finishing line long before he gets there.'

He stretched out and nodded off in the sun …

Some way behind, the tortoise lumbered along on his stubby legs. He was not fast but he was constant. He passed the sleeping hare and scurried on and on and on, all the way to the top of the mountain and victory.

When pride rides before, misfortune follows fast behind.

The Hare and the Tortoise

5

SELFISHNESS, SELF-INTEREST AND SELF-LOVE

81.

The Picarel and the Fisherman

The fisherman was out in his boat. He cast his net and pulled it in. Trapped behind the mesh was just one fish, a little picarel, a lovely little fellow, long and silver like a dart but with fins instead of feathers.

'You won't make much on me now,' said the picarel. 'Throw me back and take me later, when I'm bigger. You'll make much more that way.'

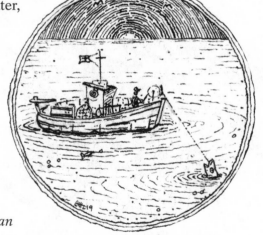

'What!' said the fisherman. 'Throw away what I have now on the promise, which isn't guaranteed, of more later? No way. Only an idiot would do that.'

Enough is better than much.

82.

The Fisherman Who Made the River Muddy

The fisherman stretched his net between the river's banks, then began to beat the water with a paddle: this was to panic the fish swimming in the river's clear, cold depths and drive them into the mesh.

A local happened to pass. He saw what was happening.

'Oi,' he said. 'You're stirring the river up – you're making it muddy.'

'So?' said the fisherman.

'But this is our drinking water,' said the local. 'You carry on like this and it won't be fit to drink. Stop it, now.'

'But I haven't had anything to eat,' said the fisherman, 'and I won't unless I do this. It's the only way to catch anything. Sorry, I can't do what you ask. Needs must.'

The belly has no conscience.

83.

The Leopard and the Fox

The leopard and the fox were arguing. Each believed he was more beautiful than the other.

'Consider our coats,' said the leopard. 'Yours is all tawny and coarse and very monotonous, whereas mine, black spots spread on a wheat-coloured base, is all variety. From which it follows, obviously, that of the two of us I am the lovelier.'

'Ah, the old beauty question,' said the fox. 'It never goes away, does it? Well, if we judge by what's on view, yes, it's true. You win. You are lovelier. But when we look into the soul what do we find? In your case, nothing except a conviction that you are the best-looking animal on earth, whereas in my case you find an intriguing mix of cunning, inventiveness and industry. From which it follows, obviously, that of the two of us I am the more appealing. Of course I am. You are empty but I have substance. And I know this to be true. One's own opinions are never wrong.'

Vanity has no greater foe than vanity.

The Leopard

The Fox

84.

The Fox Who Lost His Tail

The fox put his paw down, heard a whirring and knew … He had set off a trap …

Instinctively, the fox leapt. Dimly, he registered the clunk as the teeth closed and, at the same time, he felt a ferocious burning sensation behind.

He came back to earth. The pain was scarifying. He turned. His lovely furry brush hung from the trap's steel teeth. They had sliced it off. He was a fox without a tail.

'Oh, woe,' he cried, 'disfigured, mutilated, I will be a laughing stock.'

Over the coming weeks the fox felt his loss terribly and he was tortured by the thought that the other foxes mocked him behind his back because of what he lacked.

'Something must be done to end this misery,' he said to himself one day, 'but what?'

Then he had it.

'As my tail can't grow back,' he told himself, 'the other foxes will have to dock their tails and then we'll all be alike and I won't stand out as the only fox without a tail.'

He got all the foxes together.

'Friends,' he began. 'Once, like all of you, I had a tail. Now I don't. Am I worse off? Frankly, no. In fact, incredibly, I'm better off. Of course, I didn't know this when I had the tail. It's only now I don't have it that I've seen the light. That tail of mine was ugly, heavy, useless and it did me no favours. It slowed me down and, worse, it was a magnet for hunters. One glimpse of my brush in the undergrowth and they were after me. Since I left it behind in a trap, not one hunter has come after me – not one. So, friend foxes, cut your tails off and discover the better life without them, as I have.'

'If you still had your tail,' shouted a fox in the audience, 'would you be giving the same advice? I don't think so. You

The Fox Who Lost His Tail, part I

The Fox Who Lost His Tail, part II

haven't offered your advice to help us but because you want us all to be the same as you – foxes without tails. Well, I'm afraid we're not so gullible.'

The other foxes nodded assent and drifted away, leaving the cropped creature to nurse his hurt alone.

Wise counsel does not flow from self-interest.

85.

The Ravens and the Fearful Man

A man's country went to war. There was no standing army so every male citizen was issued with sword, spear and shield and ordered to report to the front line. The fearful man's muster point was within walking distance of his home.

The day came when he was to deploy. The man said goodbye to his family and set off. It was a bright spring morning, with empty fields stretching in every direction. When he'd gone about a mile he heard ravens' croaking.

What he'd heard, he decided, were the enemy's troops surging forward. He threw down his sword, shield and spear and froze, certain he'd see the enemy running down the road towards him at any moment. But nothing happened. The enemy did not appear. The man's terror receded. The enemy were not coming, he decided. He was safe.

He picked up his sword, shield and spear, and resumed walking. He hadn't gone more than half a dozen steps when the ravens croaked again. This time he didn't imagine this was the enemy coming.

'Croak away,' he shouted. 'You won't make a meal out of me. I won't have it.'

Fear is a great inventor.

86.

The Two Mistresses and the Middle-Aged Man

The man had not one but two mistresses, one older and one younger than himself.

The mistresses tolerated one another but the middle-aged man's hair, half-grey, half-black – that was a different matter.

The older hated the idea of having a lover who looked younger than her, so when he was with her she plucked his black hairs.

The younger hated the idea of having a lover who looked older than her, so when he was with her she plucked his white hairs.

The upshot of it all was that the man ended up with no hair and the women became the mistresses of a bald man and were ridiculed as such.

Injure others, injure yourself.

87.

The Fuller and the Charcoal Burner

A charcoal burner learnt that a fuller, who worked with cloth, cleaning and thickening it, had established himself nearby to where he lived. The charcoal burner went to see the fuller and, having made his acquaintance and finding he was an agreeable sort of fellow, suggested he should come and share his house.

'We shall get to know one another better that way,' he said, 'and, besides, because we'll be sharing, our household expenses will be halved. What do you say?'

'It's a charming idea,' said the fuller, 'but it isn't going to work. Whatever I whiten you'll blacken in no time with your charcoal soot.'

It is always easier to say no.

88.

The Lion and the Cowherd

The herdsman checked his herd. A young calf was gone.

'Keep an eye on the animals,' he said to the lad who worked with him. 'I'm away to find our stray.'

He spent the day searching the area but when dusk came he still hadn't found the missing calf. He was worried now. If the animal had simply wandered off, the herdsman reckoned, he'd have found him by this stage. That he hadn't therefore made it much more likely he'd been rustled, and that being the case, recovery was going to be much harder.

He looked up at the pale grey sky.

'Great Zeus,' he said, 'if you help me find the thief who stole my calf I vow to sacrifice a young kid-goat in thanks. You will not be disappointed.'

The herdsman had no sooner finished speaking than he heard mysterious noises coming from a nearby thicket.

'The great god has heard me,' he said. 'That must be my missing calf.'

The herdsman ran to the thicket and pushed through the growth around the edge. Once he got to the far side, he found himself in a small hidden space in the middle and face to face with a wild lion. His lost calf, half-eaten, lay in a bloody heap at the lion's feet. The lion raised his heavy head and snarled at him.

'Zeus, I vowed to sacrifice a kid if you helped me to locate the thief,' the herdsman shouted, 'but now I promise to sacrifice a bull if you get me away from the thief's claws and teeth.'

When sorrows come, they come not in single spies, but in battalions.

89.

The Dead Tree and the Ploughman

The ploughing season was approaching, and one morning the ploughman went to look at the big field he would shortly plough up. In the middle of the field there was a dead tree – withered, black, implacable. He'd always hated this tree. It produced nothing, it made the field look untidy and it was tedious having to guide the plough around it.

'Right,' he said to himself, 'there's no point just being annoyed about it. It's time to take action. I'll cut it down, that's what I'll do.'

He went home, fetched his axe and returned. He climbed the gate and began to walk across the land towards the tree. There was a spring in his step. He was whistling. He felt good. The dead tree in the middle of the field had niggled him for years but within the hour it would be felled and it would never annoy him again.

The tree was home to a host of sparrows, and the little brown birds saw the ploughman, with his axe over his shoulder, stalking towards them.

'I spy trouble,' said a sparrow.

'You're right,' the others chirruped in agreement. 'This isn't looking good. He's got an axe and he's coming right at us. It can only mean one thing ...'

The ploughman reached the tree and began to circle the trunk looking for the best place to drive his blade in.

'Don't fell this tree,' the sparrows cried out in unison. 'We'll be homeless if you do.'

'This is my land, this is my tree and it's rotten,' the ploughman shouted back at them. 'I want to cut it down, I will cut it down and that's exactly what I'm about to do. So take yourselves off. It's going to happen.'

He raised his axe and swung. The blade cut in deeply and the sparrows felt the tree tremble. There was a faint droning deep inside the trunk.

'What's that noise?' said the ploughman.

He wiggled the axe head free and saw the blade was covered in something yellowy. He dabbed his finger in the stuff then touched his tongue.

'Honey!' he shouted.

The noise inside the tree had changed from murmuring to buzzing. He knew what he was hearing now: he was hearing bees, disgruntled bees. The honey was from their hive.

The ploughman licked his blade clean, turned on his heel and headed back the way he'd come, watched by the sparrows.

Henceforth, he revered the tree because it was home to a hive that gave him honey every winter. He also never stopped feeling pleased with himself for having found it.

'Oh yes,' he said, every time he spread honey on his bread, 'how clever of me to have decided to go out with my axe that morning ...'

A man loves his own fault.

90.

The Quarrelsome Sons of the Ploughman

Throughout their childhoods the ploughman's sons bickered, sniped and fought among themselves. Their father endlessly told them to stop fighting and to start working with one another but they wouldn't listen to him. One day, his patience expended, the ploughman, remembering we live more by example than by reason, decided to try a different approach.

He summoned his sons. 'Right,' he said, 'I've a task for you lot. I want each of you to go out into the forest and fetch me a bundle of sticks and make sure your bundle is thick – plenty of twigs.'

His sons went away and returned, each carrying their bundle. The ploughman sat them down in a circle round the fire.

'Now,' he said. 'Each of you in turn will attempt to snap his bundle in half over his knee. The first lad to succeed will get a gold coin.' He had the coin ready and he showed it to them.

'So,' he said, indicating his eldest son. 'Let's see you snap your bundle in two.'

The oldest tried and failed. His bundle was too thick. All his younger brothers tried and they all failed too, and for the same reason.

'So,' said the ploughman, once every son had tried, failed and given up, 'none of you can manage, can you?'

He took his eldest son's bundle and tried to break it on his own knee.

'It's too thick, it's impossible,' he said. 'However, that is not to say it can't be done.'

He undid his oldest son's bundle and passed round a single stick from it to each of his boys.

'Right, I want each of you to break the stick you've got.'

They did.

'So do you not see?' said the ploughman. 'You can't break a whole bundle in one go but you can snap an entire bundle one stick at a time.'

'So what?' said the eldest son. 'We know that.'

'Then you must also know that if you keep on fighting,' he said, 'each of you will be broken on his own, one at a time; but stay together, like sticks in a bundle, and you won't be.'

Good sense is much matter decocted into a few words or actions.

6

GLOATING AND HEARTLESSNESS

91.

The Bramble and the Fox

The fox trotted along the top of the wall, blithe and careless, and he didn't see there was a loose stone ahead. When he put his paw on it the stone slipped sideways and began to fall earthwards. The fox began to slip too. Soon, he would be following the stone ...

But before that happened there was a moment between toppling and falling, and during this tiny instant the fox saw there was a bramble spray with coarse green leaves growing up the side of the wall and that it was right beside him.

The fox didn't think, 'That's a bramble and it won't save me,' or, 'That's a bramble and it will save me.' He just reached out and grabbed at the brown, woody tendril with his front paws. It was armed with sharp, dark thorns and as his paws slipped down it as if down a rope (for of course the spray couldn't stop him falling), the barbs sliced his pads, cutting through the calloused exterior to the softer skin underneath.

The fox landed on his back with a thump that winded him. He lay still for a second looking up at the clouds and feeling confused, then rolled deftly and was back on his paws. He let out a howl of pain and dropped onto his haunches to take the weight off his front legs. He examined his front paws one after the other. Both were bleeding.

'You didn't stop my fall *and* you made me bleed,' he shouted up at the bramble. He waved his bloody paws in the offending plant's direction, splattering dark red blobs on the ground as he did.

'What are you on about?' said the bramble. 'No one clings to me ... I do the clinging. I thought you foxes were supposed to know things like that. Perhaps you aren't as brainy as you're cracked up to be.'

You will never get from a bramble but a blackberry.

92.

The Billy-Goat and the Fox

The fox bent down to drink out of the well, lost his balance and toppled in.

'Oh, Hell's bells,' the fox said, blinking and spluttering when he surfaced.

He paddled to the side of the well to see about climbing out. Unfortunately the walls of the well, a dark, smooth stone, offered no grip. The truth sunk in. There was no way he could get out. He was trapped.

The fox trod water, waiting and listening. After a bit, the head of a billy-goat appeared over the lip of the well above.

'Hello,' said the goat, surprised and perplexed at what he was seeing – a fox swimming in the well.

'Hello,' said the fox, warm and friendly.

'You're in the well?'

'That's right.'

'Why?'

'Well,' said the fox, 'water this good you don't just drink it, you know. You actually have to be in it to really get the full benefit.'

'Really?' said the billy. He was astounded by this. 'Isn't all water just … the same?'

'Absolutely not,' said the fox. 'This here is the best in the world, superior to the water of any other well, anywhere. Come on, hop in. It'll be well worth it, you'll find. That's a pun, by the way. Well worth it? Oh, never mind. Come on. Jump in.'

'Best in the world,' said the goat. 'How can I say no?'

The goat jumped in, sank, surfaced and began to drink with great, long, noisy gulps. Yes. What he'd been told was right. The water was truly superb.

'Yes, excellent water,' said the goat when his belly was full. 'Now to get out,' he said.

He pawed the smooth stone sides with his front hooves and realised that, though getting in might have been easy, getting out would not be.

'How do we get out of here?' he asked.

'Ah,' said the fox, 'it's a problem for both of us, I think. Separately, we'll never get out of here. However, if we pull together I think we can do it.'

'Go on,' said the goat.

'The well isn't deep,' said the fox. 'You stand up on your hind legs, put your front hooves up against the wall and lift your horns as high as you can get them. I'll climb up you and get out. Then, I'll take your horns and pull you out. What do you say?'

The goat agreed. He put his hind quarters on the floor and scrambled upright. The fox clambered up his body like a ladder, got over the lip at the top and vanished from the goat's sight.

'Hey,' the goat shouted after the fox. 'We'd an arrangement. I get you out, you help me out.'

The fox came back and looked down.

'If you'd as much sense in your head as you've hairs on your chin,' he said, 'you'd have remembered what the wise man said *before* you got in: he who seeks the entrance should also think of the exit. You can ponder that while you splash about down there. Good day.'

The fox vanished again, leaving the goat in the water.

Stupidity is a hardy perennial.

93.

The Monster Mask
and the Fox

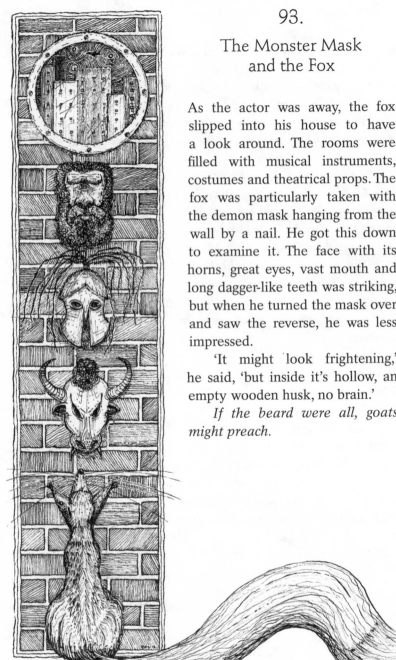

As the actor was away, the fox slipped into his house to have a look around. The rooms were filled with musical instruments, costumes and theatrical props. The fox was particularly taken with the demon mask hanging from the wall by a nail. He got this down to examine it. The face with its horns, great eyes, vast mouth and long dagger-like teeth was striking, but when he turned the mask over and saw the reverse, he was less impressed.

'It might look frightening,' he said, 'but inside it's hollow, an empty wooden husk, no brain.'

If the beard were all, goats might preach.

94.

The Drunkard and His Wife

The drunkard came home stocious and passed out before his wife, as he had often done during their long, blighted marriage.

'I've had enough of this,' said his wife. 'It's time to change.'

She carried her husband to the cemetery and locked him in a vault. 'He'll wake up and think he's dead,' she told herself walking home, 'until I reveal he isn't. He'll be shocked into sobriety.' This was her hope: a brush with mortality would result in her husband's transformation.

In the morning she returned to the cemetery and pounded on the metal door of the vault to wake her husband inside.

'Who's that?' he shouted.

'The one who brings food to the dead,' the drunkard's wife replied.

'Oh, don't bother with any food,' he said. 'Now I'm dead I can drink whenever I like and as much as I can manage. Just some wine, please.'

'The more you hope the more you suffer,' his wife howled. 'What an idiot I am …'

'What's the matter?' the husband shouted from inside the vault. 'Are you telling me you haven't any wine?'

'You were bad when alive,' his wife shouted, 'but dead you're even worse.'

Black will take no other hue.

95.

The Prophetess

'There's no god so angry,' the prophetess liked to boast, 'but my charms won't bring him round.'

Many citizens in the city believed her, sought her out and paid her handsomely for interceding with the angry gods on their behalf.

Other citizens, however, infuriated she should have reputation, wealth and status (of course they envied her), were of the contrary opinion.

'The pinnacles of high walls fall down, and the dung-heaps rise,' they raged. 'She's a witch and her magic is black.'

The authorities heard these words and understood what was being implied. They had the prophetess arrested, charged with witchcraft and hauled into the court where (it had all been fixed in advance) the judge found her guilty and sentenced her to death.

No sooner had the judge finished speaking but the prophetess was dragged off to the gallows that stood in front of the courts of justice, and everyone who'd attended her trial came out to watch her execution – which they welcomed, of course. As the hangman put the noose around the prophetess's neck, one of these good citizens shouted, 'Once you boasted no one managed the anger of the gods better than you did, yet you couldn't manage the anger of the people, could you?'

The crowd loved this. It said exactly what they felt and their delighted howls of approval were the last thing the prophetess heard on earth before the trap dropped and her neck snapped …

A few minutes later the prophetess was strung up by her feet with her dress hanging down over her face. The crowd began to disperse. Spirits were high, for not only had justice been served but there had also been that marvelous quip thrown by the citizen right at the end. It summed up their feelings in a lovely single sentence, and it wasn't often that the last word was got in like that, so perfectly and so neatly and so finally.

'Yes, a great day,' everyone in the crowd agreed, 'a great day.'

But later, lying in their beds in darkness, the image of the upside-down dangling prophetess burning before their minds' eyes, no one could sleep.

The evil which issues from the mouth falls into thy bosom.

96.

The Ox and the Heifer

The heifer, a young cow who'd yet to have a calf, stood on the edge of the track and watched the heavily laden cart, pulled by a single brown-skinned ox, crawling along towards her. Progress was slow, the load being so heavy, but eventually the ox drew near enough to hear her.

'What did you do to warrant a punishment like that load?' asked the young cow, in a solemn, moral voice. 'I'd say it must have been very bad, whatever it was.'

'She thinks I deserve this,' thought the ox, 'and I'm being punished. What is she talking about? I'm at work, that's all.'

A religious procession appeared, its followers loud, jocular and bumptious. Some of the worshippers unyoked the ox and set him free, while others threw a halter around the young cow and began to drag her in the direction of a nearby altar where they planned to slit her throat, drain her warm blood from her veins and offer it in basins to the gods.

'Heifer,' the ox shouted after the luckless cow, 'if you ever wondered why you were never put to work like me but let stand around all day, you've your answer now. You were always going to be sacrificed though you never knew it.'

That which we enjoyed for many days we pay for in one.

97.

Zeus and the Oak Trees

The oaks sent a delegate to speak to the great god.

'It seems to us that the lives we live are for nothing,' the delegate said. 'We spend decades growing up and no sooner are we done but what happens? Someone comes and chops us down.'

'Which they do using an axe with a handle made of what?' said Zeus.

The delegate said nothing.

'Seeing as you won't say, let me answer for you,' said the great god. 'They're made of oak, aren't they? So go back and tell your oaks this: one's blood kills one – you've only yourselves to blame. If you weren't so valuable to farmers and carpenters, no one would cut you down: but as you are so useful, it follows you must and will be cut down. Get over it. Now get out of my sight.'

Each man rears his own gravestone.

98.

The Wolf and the Kid-Goat on the Roof

The kid clambered onto the flat roof of the house on the edge of the village. He did this all the time.

'Seize the day,' he said, staring at the countryside, the clouds, the sky.

At that moment a wolf trotted past below.

'Hey!' the kid shouted at the wolf.

The wolf stopped, turned, yawned.

'You know, I've noticed,' said the kid, 'that all you eat are the old, the sick, the halt and the lame. Am I right?'

The wolf watched the kid-goat with his blank yellow eyes and thought how nice he would be to eat.

'Yet they say you're the top predator. Really? I don't think so. As I see it, you're actually just a thug who picks on the weak.'

'You think you're mocking me,' said the wolf, 'but you aren't. It's where you're stood that's doing the mocking.'

Place and occasion give the weak their chance.

99.

The Metal File and the Adder

Night. The blacksmith had gone home. An adder, passing the forge, seeing it shut up and knowing that meant no human being was about, slithered in through the crack under the door.

The smithy's interior smelled of horse and burnt horn. There was a hearth, a bellows, an anvil, a trough of water and a workbench. The adder wriggled his way up to the worktop where all the tools were laid out.

'Spare a bit of change for a poor hungry adder …' he said to the hammer and the pliers and the other tools.

The implements grumbled a bit but they all stumped up something for the adder, with the exception of the file.

'Ah now, come on,' said the adder, sliding over to the tall, dark tool with his long, flat face cross-hatched with cruel lines. 'Surely you can spare something for a poor old adder?'

'What are you on about?' said the file. 'I never give. I only take. I'm a file, you fool, or didn't you notice?'

A mean man is always dejected.

The Shark and the Tunny-Fish

100.

The Shark and the Tunny-Fish

The frantic tunny-fish wriggled forward, moving as fast as he was able, but it was hopeless. The shark behind him was getting closer and closer …

The tunny sensed, under his belly, the sea bed rising to meet him. He was entering shallows and he was close to land.

'Perhaps if I get up on the shore,' the tunny-fish thought (a last desperate hope this), 'I can get away from the shark.'

He surged forward desperately, hit the shelving beach and slithered forwards and upwards until he found himself stranded some way above the waterline on coarse sand, gasping. His pursuer, the shark, he saw, having followed him up the beach because of his desperate determination to kill and eat him, was lying a few feet away, also gasping for air. Out of the sea the shark could no more breathe than he could.

'Ah now,' said the tunny-fish. His life spirit was draining away. He would not live long. 'I always dreaded death. Who doesn't? But now I know that in despair there can be joy, for the cause of my dying is dying too, right beside me. Ha! Serves him right.'

There are many ways to happiness.

101.

The Fox and the Jackdaw

The jackdaw was famished. He noticed a fig tree with some hard, green unripe figs showing on it.

'I'll perch in that tree,' he said, 'and wait for the fruit to ripen. And as I'll be in the tree already, I'll get the ripe fruit before the other birds …'

The jackdaw found a place to perch. A fox passed. He noticed the jackdaw sitting quietly.

'Strange,' said the fox. 'That jackdaw usually flaps about screaming his head off. I wonder what's up with him today.'

The fox ambled over. 'You're very quiet,' said the fox.

'I am,' said the jackdaw. The bird was relieved to be perched well out of the fox's reach.

'Strange,' said the fox, 'you're just sitting doing nothing and that's not like you.'

'But I'm not doing nothing. I'm waiting.'

'What for?' said the fox. 'A mate?'

'No. For the figs to ripen.'

'And how will you survive while you wait?' asked the fox.

'Don't you worry, I'll survive. I've it all planned out.'

'Whatever the stomach is full of,' said the fox, 'with that the mouth runs over.'

'What does that mean?'

'Right now you've a belly full of hope,' said the fox, 'and it'll feed illusions, hope will, but it won't feed the body. Before those figs turn black, you're going to die, my friend, but not to worry. You'll make a nice supper for a wild dog.'

The fox turned and began to stalk off.

'I don't care what you think,' the jackdaw called. 'I'm not budging.'

He stayed where he was, and because he ate nothing his body shrank and shrank and eventually, as predicted, he died and his remains were indeed eaten by a wild dog.

Dreams give wings to fools.

102.

The Fox and the Raven

The raven spotted the open window. He flew through and found himself in the kitchen. There was a table with a plate with a juicy piece of meat on it. He grabbed the meat in his beak and flew out.

'What luck,' thought the raven.

He perched in a tree to consider, seeing as the piece was too big to gobble in one go, how to proceed.

At this very moment, as the raven was considering, a fox was passing.

'That's a nice piece he has,' said the fox. He skulked to the foot of the tree and called up, 'Hail!'

The raven heard, looked down and saw who it was. The raven detested the fox. A contemptible animal in his opinion, vicious and deceitful. 'What's he want?' he thought.

'Dear raven,' said the fox, 'there's something I've been meaning to say for a long time, and now I've run across you like this, my chance to speak is here at last.

'You are a wonderful creature. You are glossy, you are trim, you are grave, you are noble – and it has always seemed to me, because of your many virtues, that of all the birds on earth you, dear raven, are the one who should be king of the birds. Oh yes. All you lack is a voice, which, as you know, is such an important part of being the king. So there you are. No voice, the raven can't be the king.'

'What's he talking about?' the raven wondered. Without thinking he opened his beak. 'But I do have a voice …'

The meat landed softly below.

'Beware of rashness,' said the fox, putting his paw on the hunk of meat in case the raven tried to swoop in and lift it away, 'for it has been called the Mother of Regrets. If you were prudent and thought things through instead of reacting, I'd say nothing would hold you back. You would be king of the birds, for sure. But as you aren't prudent, as we see, you won't be, you'll never be.'

The fox nipped the meat between his teeth and trotted off. Sitting on his perch, the raven watched him go. It had all been going so well till he'd been lured into doing a stupid thing.

A fly cannot enter a mouth that knows how to keep silence.

103.

The Biting Dog and His Bell

The dog was a nasty, surly, bad-tempered brute who, over the years, had perfected his mode of attack. When visitors came to his master's house he would, at first, lie quietly in the corner. This was to make the visitor think he was docile and harmless. Then, once he believed the visitor thought he was not dangerous, the dog would rush up from behind and nip the back of the visitor's heels or legs. Then he'd rush away again before his victim could turn and kick him.

The dog's master tried various remedies. Sometimes after the dog had bitten someone he wouldn't feed him for a day or two, hoping in that way to get the animal to change, but hunger had no effect on him. Sometimes he'd beat the dog but that didn't work either. Sometimes he'd tie the animal up but the dog would just chew through the rope and get free. Occasionally, he even considered drowning the animal in the river, but whenever he had this idea the following thought would quickly occur: 'He's a great guard dog who'll see off any intruders, so I can't get rid of him …'

But then, having made his mind up, his thoughts would swing the other way. 'I can't have him biting my friends,' he'd think. 'That has to be stopped but what can I do? I've tried everything but nothing works.'

'Tell you what,' said his maid one day when he was complaining to her about the dog. 'Tie a bell round his neck. He'll never be able to come at anyone again without their knowing. He'll never bite again.'

The master got a bell, cornered the dog and fixed it to his neck with a collar.

'What's this?' the dog asked. He shook his head.

Clang, clang …

'Your biting days are over,' said the master.

The dog wandered out of the house and into the street.

'Hey, look at my bell,' he called to every dog he met. *Clang, clang … Clang, clang …*

An old bitch snoozing in the sun was woken by the noise.

'Look at my bell,' he called to her. 'Quite something, isn't it?'

'No,' she said. 'You've got that bell because you're a vicious biter. That's nothing to be proud off, you idiot.'

'You're just jealous you haven't got one,' he shouted back. And he swaggered on, shaking his head, ringing his bell, delighted with himself.

There is always plenty of sound from an empty barrel.

104.

The Hare and the Lion

The lion found a hare in her form, tightly curled and fast asleep.

'Dinner,' said the lion. He was about to open his vast mouth when he heard the sound of hoof-falls behind. He turned. A dun-coloured deer was moving slowly along, unaware of the lion.

The lion roared involuntarily and started after the deer. His roar woke the hare. It also alerted the deer, who started to run.

The lion chased the deer but she got away, being younger and fleeter than him. The lion stopped running once he realised he was outrun.

'I've lost the deer but never mind,' he said to himself. 'There's still the hare.'

He went back to the form. The imprint of the hare's body was still there in the grass but, of course, the hare herself was gone.

'Well, I've only myself to blame,' said the lion philosophically. 'I dropped what I had believing I had something better. Wrong. I'll know better next time.'

He is not wise who cannot sometimes be fool.

105.

The Fox, the Wolf and the Old Lion

The old lion, tired and sick, lay in his den. The news spread that he was unwell and all the animals gathered in his den and then, one after another, inquired after his health and told him how much they loved him. One animal, however, did not put in an appearance – the fox.

'Well now,' thought the wolf when he noticed this. 'Here's my chance to pay that little fiend back.'

The wolf and the fox were old enemies.

'Dear King,' said the wolf, 'our old friend, the fox, have you noticed he is not here?'

'Yes,' said the lion, 'now you come to mention it, I do.'

'But why isn't he here?' said the wolf. 'That's the question.'

'Maybe he doesn't know I'm poorly?'

'Of course he knows,' said the wolf. 'All the animals do.'

At this moment the fox slipped into the den. He was not noticed and he put up his ears to hear what was being said.

'Your Majesty,' continued the wolf, 'the fox isn't here because, unlike the rest of us, he doesn't respect you. Sir, to put it bluntly, in his eyes you are simply not worth visiting. That's why he hasn't come.'

'I'll need to nip this in the bud,' thought the fox.

The fox pushed to the front. 'Sir,' he started.

'Where have you been?' the lion shouted. 'Everyone has been to see me except you? Obviously you don't care whether I'm well or not.'

'On the contrary,' said the fox smoothly, 'I care absolutely and far more than these visitors. For while they have been here, offering kind words that won't cure you, I have been working to save you. I have scoured the world, sought out every doctor, described your appalling symptoms and now, at last, I come with a cure.'

'Really?' said the lion. 'You know how to make me better? I won't die?'

'I do. Have the pelt pealed from the wolf while he's alive and then wrap that about yourself while it's still warm. Do that and you'll live.'

'Take the wolf outside and flay him,' said the lion, 'and bring me back his pelt.'

The wolf was seized and dragged towards the den's entrance. 'Murderer,' he shouted at the fox.

'You've only yourself to blame,' the fox shouted back. 'An ox is bound with ropes and a hypocrite with words. If you hadn't slandered me, you wouldn't be in this mess.'

The forest is only burnt through its own wood.

106.

The Itinerant Priests and Their Ass

These priests, having no temple, travelled from village to village and preached either in people's homes or in public squares. Because they were peripatetic they had to bring everything they needed along with them, and to carry their possessions they had an ass, a grey, woolly, bow-backed little creature whom they kicked and whacked mercilessly as they journeyed around.

One morning, in a little village high in the mountains, the priests woke and went out to see what sort of a day it was. They found their ass lying on his side with his eyes wide open, his thick tongue sticking out and his legs rigid. He had died sometime in the night. It was exhaustion brought on by overwork combined with cruelty that had killed him.

'Well,' said the head priest, a thrifty fellow with a neat paunch, 'I say we skin him and use his pelt on our kettledrums. He'll make a great sound I'm sure.'

The priests skinned the ass, dried his pelt, then cut it into portions that they stretched over their kettledrums. The head priest's prediction was spot on. The ass's skin really did make a deep and sonorous and stirring sound …

A month later these priests met a second group of itinerant priests who asked after their ass.

'Oh, he died,' they explained.

'Enjoying a well-earned rest, is he?'

'Not at all.'

Together they walloped their drums.

'That's him,' they said. 'That's our ass. We turned him into drum skins. Now he's dead he's getting as good a thumping as when he was alive.'

'Way to go,' the others said. 'Thrash him hard!'

Some burdens you cannot escape even by dying.

107.

The Young Ant and the Young Scarab Beetle

Summer, midday, a wheat field …

A young ant, carrying a grain of wheat twice as big as herself, scurried through the stubble. She passed a young scarab beetle who was sheltering from the merciless sun below a yellow stalk.

'What are you doing, little ant, scuttling around in this heat?' asked the beetle. He had the unmannerly ways of the young.

'What do you think I'm doing?' thought the ant. 'I'm working to fill my colony's storehouse, that's what.'

As she hurried on, the beetle shouted after her, 'Suit

The Young Ant and the Young Scarab Beetle

yourself. Don't to talk to me if you don't want to. But I'll tell you this for nothing. The way you're going, you're either going to die of overwork or be fried to a crisp, or both. Ha, ha!'

Winter …

One long, dreary day the ant passed the scarab sheltering from the wind under old straw.

'All the dung is soaked and I've nothing to eat,' said the scarab.

The ant knew what she would have liked to say to him but didn't, seeing as it would only offend him.

A couple of days later the ant passed the scarab again. He was on his back, this time, with his legs sticking up in the air. There was no need to hold back now. Seeing as he was dead, there was no likelihood of offending him.

'If you'd spent the summer storing food away instead of mocking me,' said the young ant tartly, 'you'd be alive.'

She shot on, delighted with her words, harsh though they were.

If one were young twice, one would be a fool but once.

108.

The Domestic Ass and the Wild Ass

A wild ass, meandering beside a field, saw a domestic ass on the other side of the hedge, sunlight glancing off his furry back, a mouthful of grass in his square, heavy teeth.

'Hey,' the wild ass called. 'Who's looking good today, brother? That's you, I'd say, there in the middle of that lovely field, basking in the sun, chomping away, not a care in the world.'

Later the same day, the wild ass met the domestic ass again on a nearby track, and this time the domestic ass had a pair of baskets hanging over his back, both filled with heavy logs, and he was followed by a driver who was prodding his rump with a cudgel and shouting, 'Go on, you fool, go on ...'

'Well,' said the wild ass, 'I see you pay a very high price for your comforts.'

The domestic ass whinnied agreement and hobbled on.

A word is no arrow but it can pierce the heart.

109.

The Vine and the Billy-Goat

Spring. Longer days, shorter nights, warmer air. The billy-goat took himself to the vineyard, ambled up to a vine and began to nibble at the buds that would not become fruit till the autumn.

'Excuse me,' said the vine. 'What's wrong with your grass?'

'Nothing. I just prefer your fruit.'

'But it's my fruit, not yours.'

'I don't care,' said the billy-goat. 'I'm going to eat what I want.'

'I can't stop you,' said the vine, 'but don't imagine I'll provide any less wine than is needed when the time comes for your sacrifice. I'll stump up as much and more.'

The billy-goat ignored the vine's words and went on eating.

An old error has more friends than a new truth.

110.

The House-Ferret and the Parrot

A man saw a parrot with bright yellow and blue feathers in the market.

'What a specimen,' the man said.

He paid the vendor the asking price and carried the bird back to his house on his arm. Once he had his new possession inside he closed the shutters.

'There we go,' said the man to the parrot, 'liberty hall. Feel free to go wherever you want.'

The parrot flew about everywhere until eventually he landed on a shelf in a small, warm room and began squawking and screeching.

A house-ferret was asleep on the floor. The parrot's cries woke him.

'Who are you?' said the house-ferret, 'and what are you doing here?'

'I,' said the parrot, 'am your master's latest purchase and, I believe, his favourite pet, for having brought me home, he's set me free to roam wherever I want in his house.'

'What?' said the house-ferret, whose voice was as reedy and thin as the parrot's was raucous and loud. 'I don't believe it. I've lived here all my life. I make the slightest little mew, and the master will hurl something at me or chase me out of the room. But now it turns out you, who make a horrible racket, have seemingly been set free to make as much noise as you want. It's not fair.'

'Oh, dry your eyes,' said the parrot. 'Who said the world was fair? Your voice annoys, mine delights. Tough. Now buzz off. Go for a long walk and don't bother to come back.'

Nothing is too hard for the arrow to pierce when the bow is drawn with full force.

7

JEALOUSY, COVETOUSNESS AND GREED

111.

The Donkey and the Goat

The farmer kept a donkey and a goat. He fed the donkey more than the goat and she resented this.

'Why is it,' the goat would think to herself, 'since I'm as good as this donkey, that I'm not fed as well as this donkey?'

Her jealousy was huge and out of it came the following notion: epilepsy was believed to be unlucky as well as contagious; if she got the farmer to think the donkey was epileptic, he would put the donkey down. So there she had it: that's what she had to do. She had to make the farmer think his donkey had epilepsy.

She went to the donkey.

'Donkey,' she said, 'all day, every day, you're either turning the millstone or staggering around with a load on your back. My friend, if you don't get a rest soon, you're going to die. So take my advice: pretend to have a fit and throw yourself down a hole. Once you do that our master will have to give you time off. Trust me.'

The donkey did as the goat advised: he threw his head around and frothed a bit at the mouth and rolled his eyes and dropped himself down a hole. Then he got out of the hole and that was when the farmer found him. He was heavily bruised. The farmer, who valued his donkey, summoned the vet to look at him.

'He's had a bad tumble, all right,' said the vet.

'I know,' agreed the farmer, who hadn't seen the donkey pretending to fit.

'There's only one cure for injuries like these,' said the vet. 'A poultice made with goat's lung plus a month's rest.'

The farmer didn't think twice. He killed the goat, cut her

lungs out, mashed these up, made the poultice and applied it. For the next four weeks the donkey rested and at the end of the period all his bruises were gone.

One does not get crucified, one crucifies oneself.

112.

Aphrodite and the Slave Girl

The slave girl was loved by her master and he gave her dresses, jewellery, sandals, whatever she asked for. The slave girl wore her gifts, but when she studied herself in the mirror the person she saw, irrespective of how she was dressed, was plain, even ugly.

'Please, dearest goddess Aphrodite,' she would say on these occasions, 'make me alluring, make me lustrous, make me beautiful. Grant me this one wish and I promise I will honour you faithfully for the rest of my days.'

Aphrodite heard the slave girl's frequent appeals with mounting irritation and eventually, one night, she appeared to her in a dream.

'I'm so angry with that idiot, your master,' said Aphrodite, 'for believing you're beautiful. If he accepted you were ugly, as you are, that'd be different – I'd help. But seeing as he won't, you can stay exactly as you are.'

When you have enough, do not ask for more.

113.

The Crocodile and the Fox

The crocodile and the fox were arguing as to who was better. To advance his case, the crocodile stretched himself out.

'It's obvious,' said the crocodile, 'judging by this physique, that I come from a long line of top gymnasts.'

'Yes,' said the fox, 'and following their lead you've exercised so often and so hard, you've cracked your skin.'

With a lie one goes far but not back again.

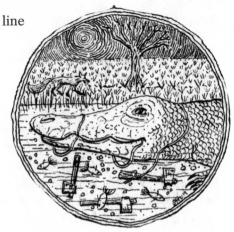

114.

The Monkey Elected King and the Fox

The monkey danced before the assembly of all the animals. His performance so delighted the delegates they all voted for him to be king – with the exception of the fox, who judged him weak, vain and deeply stupid and therefore completely unfit for the post.

Months later, mooching about the forest, the fox found a snare left by men, baited with fresh meat. He fetched the monkey to it.

'Your Majesty,' the fox said, waving at the meat, 'the moment I found this lovely morsel, I thought, "This is not for me, a mere subject. No, this belongs to my king!" So I went to find Your Majesty and led you here. Your Highness, monarch of all creatures, please, take what is rightfully yours.'

'Well, I thank you,' said the monkey. 'You are obviously a good and obedient subject and a credit to your kind. I shall not forget this.'

The monkey reached forward, grasped the meat and went to lift it. This triggered the mechanism: it snapped shut and caught his arm at the shoulder in its sharp steel teeth.

Various thoughts, ragged and disordered, now surged

through the monkey's mind. 'I'm caught. I'll never get away. I'll either die of starvation, or the hunters whose trap this is will find me alive and kill me. One way or another I'm dead, and it's all the fox's doing. He engineered this. He brought me here, he got me to reach in …'

'I've never hurt you, have I?' said the monkey to the fox. 'I've never done you any harm? So why did you do it? Why did you get me to set the trap off and precipitate my own death?'

'Why?' said the fox. 'Because you call yourself king but in fact you're no king at all. You're an idiot who doesn't think before he acts, of which the proof is that I lured you here and then I got you to reach into the trap. Only charlatans end up in the mess you're in. A real king would never find himself where you now are. That's why I did what I did.'

He who doesn't look forward falls backwards.

115.

Zeus and the First Men

The first people (those made by Prometheus) were stumbling around earth. One of these, a man, saw some other men. 'Ah,' he said, 'so that's what we are; we're bare, forked naked creatures.'

Then the man saw the bigger animals for the first time, the elephants, lions, crocodiles and wolves.

'Zeus, why is it,' he shouted, 'that the elephants, lions, crocodiles and wolves have strength, speed and power, and people don't? We're small, puny and decidedly unimpressive in comparison.'

'Do you see any animals speaking?' the great god shouted back. 'No, you don't. They can't. But you can speak, and that's the greatest gift of all. So stop with the complaining.'

'Yes, that's true,' the man thought. 'I can speak. I can take a thought and transfer it to someone else's head, even a god's, by speaking it aloud – like I just did. Yes, that is the supreme gift and now it's been pointed out to me – wow – I do feel grateful.'

And for the next while, the world was quiet because this man was grateful. But then something fresh annoyed him and up he piped again – since when, the complaining on earth has never stopped, ever.

A man's teeth often bite his own tongue.

116.

The Gold Lion and the Man Who Found It

While he was out walking the miser stumbled on a statue: it was a lion and it was made of gold.

'What do I do?' said the miser. 'Here is an incredible object, just lying around, and no owner in sight. I could just pick it up and take it home. But what if the owner discovers I have taken it and he comes after me? Or worse: what if it belongs to a god? If I take it that god will denounce me as a thief and I'll be ruined.

'I'm being torn in two here. My grabby side is shouting, "Take it!" and my craven side is shouting, "Don't touch it!" There's only one way out of this. I'll summon my servants. I'll say to *them*, "Wait until I've made myself scarce and take this home." Then I'll remove myself to a safe distance and watch them carry it away and, if there's trouble later, if the owner comes after me, I'll say, "You know what servants are like? They see something they like, they just take it. But don't worry, I'll have them whipped good and hard, so they won't be so quick to carry it off the next time they find a gold statue."'

The miser set his plan in motion and his servants carried the statue home. No one came looking for the piece but the treasure brought him no joy because now that he had it the miser was consumed by fresh terrors about robbers coming for it in the dead of night and murdering him.

Rich in gold, rich in care.

117.

Zeus, the Camel and the Bull

The camel had been watching the bull, closely.

'Because of those sharp horns of his,' the camel said, 'nobody dares push him around. On the contrary, when they go near him – *if* they go near him, that is – they're ever so polite. Well, obviously, they don't want him getting cross and goring them. Hmm ...'

The camel went and found Zeus. 'I'd like some horns,' he said.

'What on earth for?' said the great god.

'The bull has horns, and as I believe I'm entitled to have what he has, I want some too.'

'And is he asking for what you have? Is he asking for your strength, your height, your humps, your ability to live without water in the desert and to endure, in the sun and the cold, day after week after month? No, the bull is not. He's content with his gifts. But you? Oh no. You, who have so much, so much more than the bull, yet still you aren't content. Well, this'll soften your cough.'

Zeus leaned forward and cropped the top of both the camel's lovely ears, shortening them considerably.

'Next time you feel greedy, you'll remember your ears and you won't ask, I hope. Now get out of here.'

Envy eats nothing but its own heart.

118.

The Pigeons and the Jackdaw

From his perch on a tree the jackdaw could see into the aviary where the master of the house was rearing pigeons.

'Look at them,' said the jackdaw, 'plump, glossy, well-fed,

contented. All they do is sit in there and eat and preen and mate. I'd be happy to live like that ...'

A moment passed and then the jackdaw asked himself the question: 'So, you want to live like a pigeon, do you?'

And then he supplied the answer: 'Well, if that's what you want, make it happen.'

The jackdaw flew to the pit where the ashes from the fires in the house were thrown. He rolled about until he was sure he was coated with grey ash.

'And now I look like a pigeon,' he said, 'I can pass as one.'

He flew to the aviary and settled by the door. Inside the cage a pigeon saw him and called out, 'Brother, why are you out there when you could be in here, safe, well-fed, well-watered?'

The jackdaw, knowing better than to open his mouth, nodded his head as if to say, 'You are so right, friend, and I will be with you shortly, I hope.'

The master appeared, carrying a bucket of feed. He opened the aviary door and went in. The jackdaw scurried after him. Once inside, he watched the master fill a feeding tray. What was on offer? He hopped up onto the tray's edge and saw it was filled with berries, nuts and grains. Never in his life had such food ever been available for him to eat without having to make an effort.

'What a feast,' he thought. Quickened by the pure joy he felt at that moment, he opened his mouth without thinking and let out a full-throated cry. It was long, loud and raucous.

'What this?' said the master.

'He's a jackdaw,' said the pigeons.

'I've been unmasked,' the jackdaw thought. 'I won't survive. They'll kill me.'

He escaped to the garden through the open door.

The master followed. 'Be gone,' he shouted and shooed him away.

The jackdaw returned to the tree where he'd been perched just a few minutes earlier and found another jackdaw there, sitting where he'd been perched. He landed beside him.

'Hey,' said this jackdaw. 'No pigeons here. Jackdaws only.'

'But I am a jackdaw,' he said. He shook himself. A little dust came off but he remained substantially grey.

'Well, if you are,' said the other, 'you're the first grey jackdaw I've ever seen. Go on, away with you before I get a clattering here to drive you off.'

The ash-covered jackdaw flew to a mountain where no jackdaws lived and where he hoped he would be safe. He hadn't been there two hours when he was seized by an eagle and eaten.

Do not throw the arrow which will return against you.

119.

The Dogs

The master owned a black dog and a white dog. The black he trained to hunt and the white he used to guard his home.

One day the master went hunting and the black dog chased a hind and brought her down and killed her. The master carried the hind home, butchered her in his yard and cut off two pieces of meat: one he threw to the white dog and the other to the black dog.

'Not fair,' said the black dog.

'What is?' said the white dog, though he had an idea what was looming.

'I do the hard hunting work, while you stay here sleeping,' said the black dog, 'yet we both get the same reward.'

'I'd have been happy to come hunting,' said the white dog.

'That's as may be,' said the black dog. 'The thing is, you didn't.'

'And whose fault is that? Mine? No. It was our master divvied up our roles. He assigned you to hunting and me to guard duties. Or, if you prefer, he decided you'd do the work while I'd be let laze about all day. It was his plan. Go and complain to him if you like. He won't change his mind, you know.'

The black dog fell silent. The white dog had won the

argument but that didn't change anything. Inside he simmered with resentment. It just wasn't fair. Why should any meat go to him who'd done nothing to get it?

When the wagon of fortune goes well, spite and envy hang on to the wheels.

120.

The Lion and the Wolf

The wolf crept right up to the edge of the flock and seized a nice, heavy lamb between his sharp teeth and broke its neck. The terror-stricken sheep scattered and the wolf, his prey in his mouth, set off for his lair.

A lion, who had seen the whole scene, now stepped out from behind a rock and blocked the wolf's path.

'You can stop right there,' said the lion, 'and drop what you're holding.'

The wolf did as he was instructed. There was nothing else he could do. His adversary was stronger and bigger and would always prevail.

'Thank you,' said the lion, 'very obliging of you. I've always been partial to a bit of lamb, you know.'

The lion picked up the carcass and walked away.

The wolf watched the thief go. He boiled with rage.

'You know what,' the wolf shouted. 'That was mine, that was my prey and for you to take it off me, by force, just like that, is absolutely unfair. It wasn't yours to take, and it's not yours to have. What you are doing is unjust.'

The lion stopped and turned and put the carcass down.

'Unjust, really?' said the lion. 'And it was justly yours, was it? Really? The gift of a friend, perhaps? Was that what made it justly yours?'

The lion picked up the lamb's body and padded away, and as he went the wolf could hear him laughing.

There is always a rogue to rob a rogue.

121.
Zeus and the Bees

The bees went to Zeus.

'We make honey,' they began. 'And then men take our honey. They don't ask. They don't say thank you. They just assume it's theirs by right and carry it away. And year after year, that's how it's gone. Well, we're done with that. We don't want that arrangement any more. We want the right to sting anyone who approaches our hives. A few bites and men won't be quite so quick to take our honey anymore!'

'But you're bees,' said Zeus. 'You make honey. That's what I made you for. And now you come to me and say you're unhappy with your lot. You want things changed. You want the right to sting. All right, my envious little friends, I'll give you what you want. You can have your sting, just as you've demanded.'

The bees murmured. The great god was granting what they'd asked.

'But it'll be fatal – to you. You sting, you die. That's how it's going to work. So every time you go to sting a person, remember, you're going to end up dead. Yes, dead. So will it be worth it, sticking your barb into the man coming to rob your hive? Perhaps not. Now, go back where you came from, you ungrateful annoying little excrescences.'

Envy shoots at others and wounds itself.

122.
The House-Ferrets and the Mice

In the house the house-ferrets and the mice were at war. The mice were losing. They called a council of war.

'We just fight as we please, any old how,' said the most martial of the mice, a large creature with a pink nose.

'That's why we're losing. We never have a plan, we never have an objective. We're not organised. That's why the house-ferrets are destroying us. If we want to win then we need to take these steps: we appoint generals; the generals make a plan; the generals issue their orders; and the rest follow their orders. Unless we do this, we're finished. We'll be defeated.'

The mice agreed. They elected their generals by a show of hands, with the pink-nosed fellow put at the top, in overall charge. But now there was a recognition problem. The mice didn't know how to tell the generals from the rest.

'I tell you what,' said pink nose. 'We'll gather straw and make horns, which we'll tie on our heads. That way, in battle, with our white horns sticking up, we generals will be easy to locate, and the foot soldiers will know who to approach to get their orders.'

The scheme was agreed. The horns were made and fitted. Battle was joined. The generals were good but not good enough. The house-ferrets prevailed.

'Retreat,' the generals shouted. 'Back behind the wainscoting. The house-ferrets won't get us in our lairs.'

The routed mice fled towards their holes in the skirting. The foot soldiers scampered through the holes easily enough. The generals, on the other hand, on account of their straw horns, couldn't. They got stuck outside and the house-ferrets devoured them all, including the one with the pink nose.

Each one thinks much of his own wisdom, therefore the world is full of fools.

123.

The Flies and the Honey

The cat, moving through the cool cellar where all the household's food was kept, brushed against the jar of honey that

The Flies and the Honey

stood on the edge of the table. The jar fell and smashed on the stone floor. The honey it had held formed a great puddle of dark gold, with pieces of broken terracotta scattered through it.

'Honey,' shouted a fly who lived in the colony in the corner. He flew down, followed by others. They all alighted on the honey and began to feast. The stuff was delicious. And there was so much. None of the flies could stop. On and on they gorged. On and on, on and on. And the more they ate the stickier and heavier their little legs got.

Eventually, of course, the point was reached: none could eat anymore honey, though there was plenty more left. The leader fly went to leave. But what was this?

'I'm stuck,' he shouted. 'I can't move.'

Another fly tried the same manoeuvre. 'I can't either,' he said.

All the flies began to wail. They were all glued to the honey.

'Oh no,' said a third voice.

'What?'

'I'm sinking.'

'Me too …'

They were all going down and, as they all knew, once they were under, they would suffocate.

'It's the bait that tempts,' said the fly who had led the way, 'not the fisher or the rod, and now I'm dying for a moment's pleasure.'

Few are fit to be entrusted with themselves.

124.

The Butcher and the Young Men

The marketplace. Two young men stopped at a butcher's stall with trays of different meats laid out on it and sausages behind hanging from a bar.

One of the young men pointed at a sausage. 'How much?' he asked.

'Do you mean this one?' said the butcher turning.

While a conversation ensued about which sausage and how much, the second man, who wasn't talking, grabbed a handful of offal, trotters, ears and other bits, and slipped the lot into the deep side pocket of the one who was talking.

The sausage conversation ended and the butcher turned back. He realised some of his offal had been swiped while his back was turned.

'Come on,' he said, pointing at the tray. 'Put it back.'

'Put what back?' said the man who'd asked the price of the sausage.

'The offal you swiped.'

'But I haven't swiped any offal,' he said. 'What are you talking about? I couldn't have – I was talking to you.'

'Well, then *you* must have taken it,' said the butcher, pointing at the other man.

'What are you on about?' said the second man. 'Of course I haven't.' He tapped his pockets to show they were empty. 'I've just been standing here. I haven't done anything.'

'Well one of you has.'

'No, we haven't,' said the two men together. 'We haven't done anything, we promise.'

'Swear whatever you want,' said the butcher. 'Even if I can't prove it, the gods will have seen.'

The two men returned to their lodgings, roasted the stolen meat and ate it. After the meal one said to the other, 'Nothing has happened to us so far.'

'Not yet,' said the other.

'I think we got away with it.'

'We did. And no god saw.'

The real dead one must not seek in graves.

125.

Hermes and the Wood-Cutter

The wood-cutter was working on the bank of a deep river full of black water. He swung his axe at the trunk of the tree he had to fell. The blade's sharp edge struck the bark but, instead of cutting in, the axe rebounded with such force the shaft slipped out of his grip. The axe then flew into the air and dropped, plop, into the river and vanished.

'Oh no,' wailed the wood-cutter, 'my axe. What am I going do? I can't work without my axe. I can't be a wood-cutter without an axe.'

The wood-cutter sat down and began to weep. The god Hermes heard and came to see what the matter was.

'What's wrong?' said the god.

'I lost my axe in the river and now I don't know what I'm going to do. No axe, no work; no work, no money. How will I feed my family?'

'I'll get your axe back,' said Hermes, 'don't you worry.'

He dived into the river and reappeared holding an axe made of gold. 'Is this it?'

'No,' said the wood-cutter.

Hermes threw his find up onto the bank and dived again. He reappeared holding an axe made of silver. 'Is it this one?' Hermes asked.

'No.'

Hermes flung the second axe up onto the bank, dived a third time and came up holding an iron axe. 'Is this yours?'

'Yes,' said the wood-cutter, 'that's mine.'

Hermes climbed out and shook himself. 'I'm impressed,' said the god. 'When I came up with the gold axe, you could have said, "Yes, that's mine." I wouldn't have known. When I brought up the silver axe, you could have said, "Yes, that's mine." Again, I wouldn't have known. But you didn't. So you know what? They're both yours, the gold and silver. My present to you, a reward for your honesty.'

Hermes and the Wood-cutter

The god vanished. The wood-cutter went home to his village with his treasure. That night he told the villagers the story of what had happened.

'Well,' thought one of the listeners, who was also a wood-cutter, 'if that's what you do to get rich, I don't see why I shouldn't pull the same stroke.'

The following morning he went to the very spot where his newly rich fellow wood-cutter had been and threw his own axe into the river.

'Oh no,' wailed the second wood-cutter, 'my axe. What am I going do? I can't work without my axe. I can't be a wood-cutter without an axe.'

He sat down and began to weep just like the first wood-cutter. The god Hermes heard and came to see what the matter was.

'What's wrong?' said the god.

'I lost my axe in the river and now I don't know what I'm going to do. No axe, no work; no work, no money. How will I feed my family?'

'I'll get your axe back,' said Hermes, 'don't you worry.'

He dived into the river and reappeared holding an axe made of gold. 'Is this it?'

'Yes,' shouted the second wood-cutter. 'That's it, that's my axe.'

'You know,' said Hermes, 'I had this same experience yesterday … a wood-cutter like you lost his axe in the river, only that wood-cutter said, no, his axe wasn't a gold one, it was an iron one, and today I'm wondering if it's the same story again.'

The wood-cutter's face reddened.

'This is yours, isn't it?' The lesser god produced the man's iron axe, which he had in his other hand. 'You know,' said Hermes, 'because of what you did and the way you tried to trick me, you're not getting either.'

The lesser god hurled both axes into the middle of the river, climbed out onto the bank and vanished.

Wealth makes wit waver.

126.

The Floating Tree and the Travellers

A party of travellers were on the coast walking towards the city. They'd been walking for a long time and they were tired and they still had a long way to go. The sun was high. In the distance, far out at sea, something large was floating towards them, borne in by the tide. The travellers stopped to look at it.

'What do you think that is?' asked one.

'A ship?' asked a second.

'Could be,' said a third.

'You know,' said the first, 'I think it is a ship, a warship, and it's heading for the city, I bet, like us.'

The harder they looked the more the travellers were convinced that what they saw was a warship.

'I say we wait for it,' someone proposed. 'I'm sure they'll give us a lift to the city. Can you imagine how lovely to float there instead of tramping in this heat?'

The travellers agreed to wait. Time passed. What they were seeing grew closer.

'I don't think it's a warship,' said the speaker who had been first to spot something far out at sea.

'You're right, it doesn't look like a warship,' said the second.

'It's a merchant ship,' said the third.

'Yes, that's exactly what it is,' said the first.

The harder they looked the more the travellers were convinced that what they saw was a merchant ship.

'Well,' said another, 'still worth waiting for, I say. We'll still get a lift.'

The travellers agreed. They waited. The sea shimmered. The sun beat down. The object got closer and closer and then it came really close and they saw that it was not a vessel but a tree, a whole tree, with all its branches, leaves and roots.

'We are often shot with our own feathers,' said the first speaker.

'Man's greatest enemy is his own opinion,' said the second.
'What a man looks for he finds,' said the third.
'Come on,' said someone else, 'we fools had better go.'
The travellers trudged on.
Doubt even your eyes, still less trust other people's words.

127.

The Ass and the Mule

The ass and the mule were labouring side by side up the mountain. The little ass found the going really hard.

'We're carrying the same weight,' said the ass to the mule, panting as he spoke, 'but that isn't right. Seeing as you're bigger and stronger, you should be carrying much more.'

A bit further on the ass stumbled and stopped. He really was exhausted. The driver shifted half his load to the mule.

'Go on,' the driver shouted and he goaded the animals forward. The path grew steeper. The ass found the going even harder. Eventually he stumbled and stopped a second time. The driver prodded and pulled but the ass would not budge. The driver shifted the rest of his load to the mule.

'So, if this is how it's going to be,' said the mule, 'don't you think in the interests of fairness I should now get twice as much to eat?'

Everyone rakes the embers to his own cake.

128.

The Ass and the Lapdog

The master owned an ass and a Maltese terrier. The ass lived in a stall in the stable and every day the stable boy cleaned his stall and gave him hay and water and combed his coat. It was about as good a life as an ass might expect.

The terrier lived in the master's house. He sat at the master's feet when he was dining and the master would throw him little titbits from his plate. He sat on the master's lap when the master sat in front of the fire in the evening. He slept on the master's bed alongside the master at night.

'It's not fair,' said the ass one day, 'that I live like I do while that little dog lives like he does. I'm just as loyal to the master and I do as much for him as that dog. I should sit at the master's feet when he's dining and receive little titbits from his plate. I should sit on the master's lap when he sits in front of the fire. I should sleep on the master's bed at night. Of course I should.'

The ass heard his master's footsteps. He was a cunning animal. With his nose, he nudged open the bolt on his stall and got out. Then he ran up to his master.

'Why aren't you in your stall?' said the master. 'Come on, I'm going to put you back.'

The ass stood quietly. His master grabbed his mane. The ass turned his head and began to rub his big thick tongue up and down his master's face. He had seen the little dog do this and he knew the master loved it.

'What are you doing?' the master shouted. 'Stop it, you vile animal. I don't want your loathsome drool all over me.'

At that moment the stable boy, having heard the commotion, came to see what was happening.

'Hey,' said the master. 'Take this imbecilic animal back to his stall, will you, and give him a thrashing? He thinks he's a bloody dog but we'll soon beat that idea out of him.'

No one deceives us more than our own thoughts.

The Ass and the Lapdog

129.

The Cicada and the Ass

The ass heard the raw, slow, mesmeric chirping of a cicada.

'Incredible,' said the ass. 'I want to sing like that.'

The ass went and found the insect.

'I presume what you eat is what gives you that incredible voice of yours,' said the ass.

'Maybe,' said the cicada.

'So what do you eat?'

'Dew.'

'Dew?'

'Yes, the moisture that covers the earth at dawn,' said the cicada.

'Well,' said the ass, 'if that's how to get that voice then I'll only eat dew from now on.'

And that's what he did. From then on he took nothing but the dew he licked off rocks and plants until he died.

Crave for nothing, grasp at nothing.

130.

The Cranes and the Wild Geese

The cranes and the geese were foraging together on wet ground. The cranes ate small mouthfuls. The geese gobbled huge mouthfuls. The birds heard hunters coming, splashing as they came. The shout went up. 'The hunters are coming ...'

The cranes folded out their long, delicate wings, rose lightly into the grey sky and were gone before any harm could come to them. The geese stretched their sturdy and strong wings and beat them up and down, producing a sound like dry leather being bent first this way and then that. However, despite this effort, and the effort was huge, they could not get their heavy white bodies, weighted down as they were by their full bellies, to lift into the air. Then the hunters came up, threw their nets over them and wrung their necks. They ate them that night.

A fish dies by its open mouth.

8

CUNNING, GUILE AND INSIGHT

131.

The Eagle and the Two Captors

The hunter netted an eagle. 'What a prize,' he said. He got his shears.

'You'll live with my hens,' he told his captive as he set about clipping his wings. 'You're feathered, they're feathered, so you'll all get on, won't you?'

The great bird was too depressed to speak. First caught, then shorn, his life was finished.

The hunter carried the eagle home in a sack.

'Home sweet home,' said the hunter as he approached his hen-house. He opened the hen-house door. The hens roosting on their boxes looked up and saw their master come in.

'What have we here?' they asked.

Their master up-ended the sack and tipped the eagle onto the hen-house floor. Then he backed away and shut the door behind him. The chickens clucked loudly. This was all very strange.

'Who are you?' the hens asked the eagle.

'A trophy,' said the eagle glumly.

'We don't do trophies here,' said the hens. 'We're working hens. Get laying.'

'Once I was a magnificent wild creature,' said the eagle. 'Now I'm a prisoner lying on the floor of a hen-house on a stinking mix of straw and droppings. Well, I won't be eating or drinking. I intend to lie here till I die. Nothing else I can do.'

'As you wish,' said the hens. 'It's your lookout.'

Over the following days the eagle shrank towards death. At first his new master shouted and stamped his feet. 'You must eat,' he said. 'You must drink.'

By day three, however, he'd come to realise the eagle would never relent.

'He's just going to lie there in the filth, refusing to eat or drink, until he dies,' he said. This was to himself rather than the hens but they heard him anyway. 'And frankly,' he continued, 'I'm sick of the sight of the wretch expiring on the hen-house floor. I've had enough. He can die on someone else's watch. They can have his death on their conscience.'

'Way to go,' said the hens, who were as tired of the eagle moping about as their owner was. 'Let someone else deal with him.'

The hunter put out the word. The eagle in his hen-house was for sale. A neighbour made an offer and he accepted the price without haggling. He wanted the eagle gone.

The new owner carried his purchase home and rubbed myrrh on the sore places on his bare wings. 'This will make your feathers regrow,' he said, 'and once they're back I don't expect you to stay. You'll be free to fly away.'

The eagle resumed eating and drinking … time passed … his feathers grew … and finally the day came when he was ready to fly. He spread his vast wings and rose into the clouds and then, circling round, he stared down at the ground far below. Ecstasy. He spotted a plump hare, a miniscule spot in the vast landscape. He swooped and grabbed it with his talons, carried it back and dropped it at the feet of his benevolent second owner.

A fox witnessed this and sought the eagle out later. 'You made a big mistake there,' said the fox. 'It's not your second master who should have got your gift but the first one.'

'What?' said the eagle. 'My first master punished me: he clipped my feathers and imprisoned me in his nasty hen-house. The second saved me from the first man *and* restored my feathers *and* let me go, so obviously he's the one who deserves the gift, duh.'

'No, wrong,' said the fox. 'He's already good and your gift won't change that. But if the first had got the hare, I'd say that'd put him off trapping you and clipping your wings next time he has you at his mercy, duh!'

Sometimes you must appease not the good but the bad.

132.

The Swallow and the Nightingale

The swallow flew to the wood to put a proposal to his old friend the nightingale.

'Why are you living out here in a tree,' he said, 'when you could be in the village under the eave of a house, like me? It would be warmer, drier and I'd see you more often.'

'It would,' said the nightingale, 'but the trouble is, they eat us. I live among people and within a week my tongue would be in a pan simmering in butter, and my flesh would be under a pie-crust baking in the oven. At least out here they have to come and catch me first if they want to eat me, and I don't make that easy. Oh yes, here's the place to live.'

Do not stand in a place of danger trusting in miracles.

133.

The Mice and the Cat

The nest of mice lived in an empty old house, bothering nobody.

One day a cat climbed through a broken window and got into the kitchen.

'I say!' said the cat. There were mice wherever he looked. 'Paradise …'

Snap, snap, snap, the cat went to work. The kitchen was filled with sound: the thudding of the cat's paws on

the floor, the high-pitched screams of the mice he caught as he tore them to pieces and the piteous cries of the mice who escaped as they squeezed behind the wainscoting. Then the carnage was over and the room was still ...

Behind a dingy stretch of skirting board, crouched in the dark in a space that smelled of brick mould, one mouse cowered, his ears straining. He heard a bit of scuffling and some sliding that made no sense to him, following which – nothing.

'What is going on out there?' he thought.

The mouse squinted through a tiny gap. He saw the floorboards with dead mice strewn everywhere, their mouths open, their eyes glassy, little red pools around their heads. He saw the legs of the kitchen table. He saw the pipe running down from the stone sink. He saw the panelled wall with its line of pegs, a basket dangling from one, an apron from a second, a sunhat from a third and ...

'What's that hanging from the fourth peg?' thought the mouse. 'My God, it's the cat waiting for the survivors to think he's gone and then come out thinking they're safe – at which point he'll drop to the floor and pounce.'

'Hey, you, hanging from the peg,' he shouted, 'don't think I'm taken in. No, mate, I see you, I know you and I'm not coming out for you to get me.'

Other survivors heard this and started to chant, 'We're not coming out ...'

'They're not coming out,' thought the cat. 'No point hanging on then.'

He dropped to the floor and jumped up onto the window ledge.

'Don't worry, I'll be back,' he said, and he vanished through the window he'd come in by.

The mice buried their dead and by nightfall the house was empty: they'd all gone.

Fear teaches how to run.

134.

The Wild Goats and the Goatherd

An autumn evening. Wind, dirty cloud, a feeling the weather was on the turn.

The goatherd went out to fetch his herd in for the night and saw that his domesticated animals had been joined by a tribe of wild goats.

'They must know something about the weather,' he said.

He drove all the animals, wild and domesticated, into a cave for the night.

The next morning an atrocious storm blew up, and as the animals couldn't possibly go out the goatherd fed them. He gave each of his own animals just a handful of fodder, enough to see them through the day: but to each of the wild ones he gave an armful. His reason for the large ration was obvious: he wanted them to stay.

The next day came. No wind, a milky sky. The goatherd drove all the goats to a high pasture. No sooner were they through the gate and into the field but his own goats began to tear at the grass. They were hungry, of course, on account of having had so little to eat the previous day. The other goats, the wild ones, did not even nibble at the grass but turned and began to head up the mountain.

'Hey,' the goatherd called. 'What are doing? You can't go, not after how I looked after you yesterday, all that food and everything.'

One of the wild goats stopped, turned and spoke. 'You treated us better than your own, thinking to keep us. But that only taught us that if more goats came along you'd happily neglect us for them.'

Experience is the teacher of life.

135.

The Tunny-Fish and the Fisherman

The fisherman sat in his boat which floated out at sea. His day hadn't gone well and his mood was low.

'My lines aren't fouled,' he said, 'my hooks are sharp, my bait's perfect, yet not even one bite have I had from dawn to now. It's not fair.'

On the edge of his vision he saw something happening out to the side. There were white sprays of foam; something had broken the surface.

The fisherman turned to look. The commotion was caused by two great fish, one chasing after the other. Closer and closer they came and then they were close enough that he was able to see the pursued was a tunny-fish, plump and dense and lovely, and the pursuer was a shark, sleek and black, his fin jutting up like a pennant. Closer and closer they came, and clearer and clearer it became that they were coming towards him, heading right at his boat.

'They'll go under me, surely,' he said. Well, no and yes …

When he was so close the fisherman could have reached out and touched him, the tunny jumped out of the sea, obviously intending to fly over the boat; but then he faltered, lost power, flopped down and landed – bang! – in the bottom of the boat, right in front of him.

The next instant the shark plunged down, obviously intending to swim under the boat.

'Incredible,' the fisherman said, feeling the shark bumping below, his rough skin dragging like sandpaper across the bottom timbers of the keel.

On the other side of his boat, the shark reappeared, speeding onwards, baffled, with no quarry to chase.

Meanwhile the tunny lay wriggling and twitching, his gills frantically opening and closing as his life force slipped away. Then the tunny stopped moving. The fisherman touched his side, cold, clean, salt-encrusted. It was a good animal, heavy, weighty.

'You'll fetch a good price,' the fisherman said and he was right. He got an excellent price from a merchant on the quayside.

A boundless bitter sea: but turn your head and there is the shore.

136.

The Sun and the North Wind

The north wind and the sun were in dispute.

'I am stronger than you,' said the wind.

'No,' said the sun. 'You might rush about and make a lot of noise, but when push comes to shove, I'm infinitely stronger.'

'I tell you what,' said the wind. 'See that fellow.' He indicated a traveller walking along a dirt road below. 'The first to strip off his clothes is the stronger.'

The wager agreed the wind went first. He howled and blew and the traveller froze. He pulled on a second shirt, a scarf, a jacket and finally an extra cloak on top of the one he was already wearing. The wind pummelled the traveller even more frantically, hoping with his fierce force to blow it all away, everything the man had on. But of course it went the other way: the man got colder, and the longer that went on, the tighter he pulled his clothes to keep himself warm in the gale he found himself in.

'Not much success,' said the sun. 'My turn now.'

He shone moderately. No rush, no bustle, just quiet, steady warmth. The extra cloak came off. The sun increased his heat slowly. The other cloak came off. Now the sun gradually turned the heat right up until he was beating down ferociously. The traveller began to sweat. The jacket, the scarf, the second shirt came off. The air was now so hot it hurt the man to breathe. He heard the sound of a river. The sun had

The Sun and the North Wind

Death and the Old Man

timed it so he'd be sweltering at the moment he heard the sound the river made.

The traveller left the track and went to the bank. The water, so clear and cold and inviting, was exactly what he needed at this moment. Heaven sent. The traveller undressed and slipped in. The sun, seeing the red-skinned traveller splashing in the shallows, chirped to the north wind, 'See – persuasion is better than force.'

Drive slowly, you will get further.

137.

Death and the Old Man

One winter's day the old man went to the forest for firewood. He chopped up what he needed, lashed the lengths into a huge bundle and heaved this onto his back. The weight was insupportable.

He threw the bundle down. 'That's it,' said the old man. 'I've had enough struggle and toil for one life. I've come to the end.'

He sat down on his bundle. 'Death,' he shouted. 'Where are you when you're wanted? Come here.'

Death appeared from the trees, tall, young, slightly round-shouldered, with pale blue eyes and soft hands.

'What can I do for you?' said Death in his pleasant, even, beguiling voice.

It was one thing to imagine Death but to see him in the flesh, ready to act, that was a different matter. 'Not wanting to live is not the same as wanting to die,' the old man thought.

'I dropped my bundle,' the old man said quickly. He stood up. 'You wouldn't give us a hand to get it back up on my shoulders, would you?'

At a distance the ideal's a marvel; closer the reverse.

138.

The Eagle and the Ploughman

The ploughman heard something as he plodded along. He went to see. It was an eagle trapped in a net.

'I'll cut you free,' said the ploughman, and he cut the mesh open with his knife and the eagle flew off.

Days later, the ploughman rested against a high stone wall warmed by the sun.

In the sky above, wide, clean and blue, the eagle the ploughman had cut loose trailed slowly along, gazing down. He saw the wall, he saw the ploughman, he saw the future.

The eagle dropped straight down with great speed and total precision. Before the ploughman even knew it, the eagle had snatched his headband off his head with his sharp beak. Then he swooped off and landed on a rock just a few feet away.

'Hey, my headband.' The ploughman stood up and started towards the eagle. 'I cut you free and this is how you pay me back?'

The eagle skittered a few feet further and waggled his head, shaking the headband.

'This is a joke, is it? Ha, ha, ha … Look, I'm laughing.'

He advanced. The eagle retreated.

'Ah ha. This is a game. I see …' The ploughman heard a strange rumbling and wrenching noise behind. He turned without thinking and saw a great cloud of dun-coloured dust and an untidy heap of stones where the wall against which he'd been leaning only a few moments before had been.

'My lord,' said the ploughman, 'I'd have been under that rubble if I'd been sitting there. I'd be dead.'

He turned back. There was his headband, a neat circle on a rock. He looked up. The eagle was a small black speck high in the sky.

He who sows kindness reaps gratitude.

139.

The Dogs and the Ploughman

Deepest winter. The small farmhouse high in the mountains was buried in snow, and the ploughman who lived there could not get away to the valley below for food.

'Well,' he said, 'it's me or the sheep.'

After he'd eaten the sheep he said, 'Nothing else for it, it'll have to be the goats.'

And once the goats were eaten, he said, sharpening his knife on a whetstone, 'It grieves me but it'll have to be the oxen next.'

The ploughman's dogs, who had watched every animal being eaten and were watching now as the ploughman ran his finger along his blade to see if it was sharp enough to cut his oxen's throats, looked to one another.

'Once he eats his oxen,' said an old black and white collie, 'it's obvious who'll be next.'

'Yes, us. Oh, how truth pricks the eye,' said the red bitch. 'Time to run.'

The dogs slipped out silently and fled across the snow.

No worse pestilence than a familiar enemy.

140.

Demades the Orator

Demades realised no one in the assembly hall was listening to his very important speech.

'Well, if you don't like what I'm saying,' he said, 'what would you like to hear about?'

'What about one of Aesop's fables?' shouted someone in the crowd.

'Done,' the orator said. He drew himself up. 'The goddess Demeter, an eel and a swallow are travelling together

– unlikely as it seems, I know – and they come to the bank of a wide, fast-flowing river. The swallow soars up, the eel plunges forwards and …'

He stopped. The crowd grew restless. Some shuffled. Some coughed. What was this? Why wasn't he saying anything?

'And … go on,' shouted the man who'd asked for the fable in the first place. 'What about Demeter? What did she do?' The crowd were relieved by the question. They burned to know as much as he did.

'What did she do?' said Demades. 'You want to know? She turned and she said, "How many times have I told you? The work of today, do not leave for tomorrow. You should not be listening to one of Aesop's fables while thinking we'll do the hard work another time. You should be listening, right now, to what Demades has to say to you about the government of your city and the threats posed by your enemies."'

The men closest to the man who had asked for the fable muttered at him. 'What were you thinking? We haven't time to be listening to stories. We've got more important things to worry about,' they said, while elsewhere in the crowd citizens cried, 'Go on, Demades, get on with the business in hand.'

Let the folly of others be your wisdom.

141.

Hermes and the Artisans

'Hermes, I want you to carry the poison of lies down to earth,' said Zeus, 'and I want you to spread it over every haberdasher and greengrocer, every butcher and baker and candlestick maker and every other artisan too, while you're at it. They'll never thrive if they don't lie, so we have to make certain they can and, what's more, that they're good at it. So, lesser god, get to work …'

Hermes ground the poison of lies into a paste in his mortar with his pestle, taking care that he made plenty. When it came to the poison of lies, he reckoned he couldn't have enough. Then Hermes carried the vile unguent to earth and went about daubing every man and woman in the artisanal line. Finally, when he'd only the horse-dealer left to anoint, Hermes found the amount of poison he'd left was more than any other single person had had spread on them.

'Hmm,' said Hermes, 'there's no point wasting any of this stuff, is there? No, there certainly isn't ...'

He smeared all he had left on the horse-dealer and, since that day, though every artisan is a competent liar, none of them lie like horse-dealers or their descendants in the motor trade.

Where goes the needle, there goes the thread.

142.

The Belly and the Feet

The belly and the feet were wrangling.

'I'm clearly the supreme organ,' said the belly.

'How do you work that out?' said the feet, both speaking together.

'I take the wine, the olives, the bread, the cheese and everything else that comes in,' said the belly, 'and I send it to wherever it's needed, which keeps the tongue talking, the eyes seeing, the nose smelling and so on. So you'd do well to remember when you consider who's more important that you wouldn't be going anywhere if I didn't feed you.'

The feet were feeling bad tempered already, having been stood on all day, and now the belly was coming out with this tripe.

'What are you talking about?' said the feet. 'You don't actually do anything. You just wait, the food and drink comes, you digest it all, and that's it.'

'No, that's not it,' said the belly. 'I'm the great disburser who selflessly sends everything on to where it's needed. Without me, you'd be dead.'

'No,' said the feet in unison, '*we* take you to the food and drink. Without us, you'd be dead.'

One has too much, another has too little but nobody ever has just enough.

143.

The Bitten Traveller

The traveller was on a road. It was a spring day. Stone walls to left and right, and inside the walls, small fields of bright green grass. Clouds in the sky, huge and swollen. A lark high overhead, its pure, clean voice filling the warm air.

The traveller heard scratching behind. Something was approaching him at incredible speed. He turned and saw it was a dog, black and white, belly low to the ground, lips lifted, teeth bared, streaking forwards and almost on him.

The man raised his stick, but before he could bring it down the dog fastened on his ankle and bit down through his skin. The dog drove his teeth all the way to his bone. Agony …

'Ah!' the traveller shouted.

He whacked the dog on its ribs. The animal let him go, yelped and veered off.

The traveller swiped again and caught the dog's rump. Another squeal. The dog raced off to a nearby gate. He wriggled through the bars and vanished into the field beyond.

The traveller's wound throbbed. He peered down at it. On his ankle, blood blooming and wet flowing.

'That's bad,' he said. 'How am I going to stop this?'

At that moment a man appeared, as if out of nowhere, coming the other way to the one the traveller had been heading. He drew level with the traveller, stopped and peered down at his foot.

'Was you bit?' said the apparition.

'I was,' said the traveller.

'The mutt run off then?'

'He went through that gate.' The traveller pointed at the gate in question with his stick. 'I need to stop the bleeding,' said the traveller. 'Would you have a bit of rag or something?'

'I've better than a rag,' said the man. 'I've a way to stop that bleeding altogether.'

'Really, how?'

The man pulled a piece of bread from his pocket. 'You wipe your blood with that and you go after that dog and you throw it to him to eat and he eats it and that's you back to how you was.'

'You mean,' said the traveller, 'that's my bite gone? No bleeding, nothing, my skin back to the way it was?'

'Absolutely,' the man said. 'Let me wipe your bite and then we'll go into the field after the blaggard. He won't have gone far. Come on, put your leg out.'

'I don't think so,' said the traveller. 'I try that carry-on of yours and you know what?'

'What?'

'Every dog in the country will be after me. All the dogs will be going, "I get a bite out of him, I'll get a lovely bit of bloody bread as a reward."'

The only cure for idiocy is no.

144.

The Cock, the Dog and the Fox

As they were great friends, the cock and the dog set out together on a journey. As dusk fell at the end of the first day they found themselves in a dark wood.

'We need somewhere secure to sleep for the night,' said the dog.

'How about here?' said the cock. He nodded at a tall blasted oak, quite dead. Its trunk was hollow and its boughs were thick.

'Ideal,' the dog said.

The dog wriggled through a hole into the tree's hollow centre and lay down on the floor strewn with flakes of old dry wood that smelled of mushroom, while the cock flew up and found a perfect perch for the night to roost in a 'V' made by two branches.

'An excellent berth, my friend,' the dog called up to the cock.

'Thank you,' the cock called down.

They both went to sleep …

The night passed without incident. Morning came. Grey pearly light filtered through the leaf canopy of the trees all around. The cock woke. He saw the light.

'I may not be at home but still,' he said, 'that's no reason not to start as I always doo.'

He tilted his head, opened his beak and produced a long, lusty, 'Cock-a-doodle-doo.'

Nearby, in his hide, a fox who had just woken himself heard the crowing.

'A cock,' said the fox, 'in my wood?' He rose and stretched. 'What's he doing here?'

Again, 'Cock-a-doodle-doo,' for this cock would never settle for just one iteration. Three were his minimum.

'I think my breakfast has arrived,' said the fox, 'and he's just called to tell me he's ready.'

The fox came out of his hide.

'Cock-a-doodle-doo …'

'Right,' said the fox. 'He's at the dead oak.'

He sallied over to the tree and found the cock sitting where he'd spent the night. The bird was preening himself.

'Was it your "Cock-a-doodle-doo" I just heard booming through the woods?' said the fox.

'Yes,' said the cock. He was glad he was where he was and not down below where the russet-coloured, sharp-toothed fox stood.

'Yours is not the first cock's crow I've heard,' said the fox. 'I've heard many in my time. But yours was definitely the most sonorous and the most beautiful I've ever encountered. I would love to make your acquaintance. Can I entice you to join me here below?'

'I can do better than that,' said the cock. 'Go to the door – that's the gap in the trunk – and wake the doorman. He'll show you the way up.'

'I'm in,' murmured the fox. 'Breakfast here I come.' He jumped through the hole in the trunk and landed on the dog, who was still asleep but now woke instantly, sprang up instinctively, got his jaw around the intruder's throat and didn't let go until the fox was dead.

He has an incurable disease who believes all he hears.

145.

The Wild Ass and the Lion

The wild ass saw the lion. His pelt was dun and his huge mane was brown and he was lying on his side in the shade of a rock, his legs stretched out, the black pads of his paws showing. He was asleep. He looked contented.

'I wonder would I like his life better than mine?' said the ass. There was only one way to answer this question. 'I'll shadow him and see,' said the ass.

The ass shadowed the lion that day and the next day and the one after. By the evening of the third day he had his answer.

'When the lion's hungry,' said the ass, 'he finds some animal's spoor, tracks it down, kills it and eats it. Otherwise, he spends his days sleeping or frolicking with his pride. My life couldn't be more different. All day, every day, I spend roaming about looking for grasses and bushes to graze on. I hardly sleep and never see a female. It's obvious whose life is better – it's his! So I'm going to ask if we can be allies, if I can join him and be with him and live like him. Of course, it'll mean a shift from grass to meat, but I can't see that's going to make much difference.'

The ass went to the lion.

'I'm only a wild ass,' he said, 'but I can be fast when needs be and I'm cunning, and I'd like to make a suggestion. We hunt as a pair: you with your strength and I with my speed – we'll be an incredible combination. No animal will be able to elude us.'

'If you wish,' said the lion. 'Let's give it a go.'

The next day they sallied out together. First they caught a sow, a young heavy creature with plenty of meat; then a wild stallion who nearly outran them only they trapped him on a dry riverbed and he couldn't get away; then they killed a couple of young antelopes; and finally they took a dog and a fox. The hunting part over, they gathered their spoils together and the lion, whose technique was quick and brutal, divided each carcass into three equal portions.

'As I am king of the beasts,' said the lion, 'I take the first portion, as is only right and proper. Then there's the share to which I'm entitled as a partner in this joint enterprise, the second portion. So I have that too. And then, finally, we come to the third part, which, unless it comes to me, will be the occasion of great harm to you. Do you understand?'

The ass understood perfectly well and he nodded to show that he offered no objection. Of course not. That would have angered the lion, which wouldn't have been healthy for him.

'Isn't it nice we understand one another so well?' said the lion. 'Thank you for your help. Off you go now. There's a good ass!'

The ass clumped away, his head hanging down.

He who warms himself at a fire should know that it burns.

146.

The Lamb and the Wolf

The lamb ran, the wolf chasing behind her. A temple loomed up. The lamb ran up the steps and disappeared through the temple's doorway.

The wolf went to the bottom of the steps but he was disinclined to go further in case people came out or he was seen, which, either way, would be fatal for him.

'Hey,' the wolf shouted after her. 'Little lamb.'

The lamb, who'd heard the wolf calling, put her small black nose round the lintel of the door she'd gone in through, but that was as much of herself as she'd show him.

'Don't stay in there,' said the wolf. 'You might think it's safe but it isn't. There's a sacrificer in there, same as every temple, and as soon as he sees you, you know what he'll do? He'll grab your legs, carry you to the altar, cut your thin woolly throat and offer your warm blood to some distant god. Don't hang about. Get out of there while you can.'

'He who speaks much must either know a lot or lie a lot,' said the lamb, 'so if it's all the same to you, I think I'll stay where I am. I could be wrong but, frankly, I'd rather be sacrificed than be eaten by you.'

Even a bad coin must have two sides.

147.

The Ewe and the Injured Wolf

The wolf lay close to the stone wall, out of the sun, eyes shut tight. He had been badly mauled by dogs, was covered in huge scabs and was widely assumed by the sheep grazing nearby, because he was so very still, to be dead.

Then the wolf lifted first one eyelid and then the other and his ominous yellow eyes flashed into life.

'Little ewe,' he called, to the sheep closest.

She turned, carefully, and angled her head to listen, while thinking, 'Do I run?'

'I'm incredibly thirsty, little ewe,' said the wolf. 'There's a stream at the bottom of the field. I would count it a great kindness and I would be forever in your debt if you could fetch me something to drink, kind little ewe.'

'Get you water?' said the ewe.

'Yes,' said the wolf. 'I can manage about the meat, my dear, if I can only get a little something to drink.'

'I'm sure you're right there,' said the ewe, who was both quick and wary. 'If I bring you water you'll have absolutely no difficulty about the meat. Good day.'

The ewe turned and hurried off in the direction of the flock, shouting as she went, 'He isn't as dead as he looked.'

He who sells poison uses a flowery sign.

148.

The House-Ferrets and the Bat

The bat was hanging upside down from the thin branch of a pine tree at the bottom of the garden when it let go and fell to the pine-needle-covered floor below.

The house-ferret from a nearby house saw the bat fall and ran over and put a paw on one of her thin-boned wings before she could recover her senses and fly back up into the tree.

'You're not going to kill me, are you?' said the bat.

'Of course, what else?' said the ferret. 'You're a bird, I'm a ferret and that's how it goes. We're enemies. When a ferret gets a bird, of course he kills it. Always.'

'But I'm not a bird,' said the bat. 'Look at me. Do I have feathers?'

'No,' the ferret agreed, not really liking what he was hearing.

'And I'm furry, aren't I?'

'Yes,' said the ferret.

'And that's because I'm really a mouse.'

'A mouse?'

'Yes, a mouse.'

'A mouse?'

'Yes.'

'You promise?'

'I'm a mouse, I promise, a mouse who lives in a tree and happens to have wings as my kind do.'

The ferret took his paw away. 'Well, seeing as you're not a bird,' he said, 'seeing as you're a mouse, I'd better let you go ...'

Another day, the same bat fell from the same tree and landed in the same garden. A house-ferret from another nearby house saw what had happened and ran over to the bat sprawled on the pine needles and put his paw on her bony wing.

'You're not going to kill me, are you?' said the bat.

'Of course, what else?' said this ferret. 'You're a mouse, I'm a ferret and that's how it goes. We're enemies. When a ferret gets a mouse, of course he kills it. Always.'

'But I'm not a mouse,' said the bat. 'Look at me. Do I have a tail?'

'No,' the ferret agreed, not really liking what he was hearing.

'And I have wings. You're standing on one. Have you ever seen a mouse with wings?'

'Ah, no,' said the ferret.

'And do you know why I have wings?'

'No.'

'Because I'm a bird.'

'Really?'

'Birds have wings and I'm a bird.'

'You're a bird?'

'Yes.'

'You promise?'

'I'm a bird. I promise.'

216

The ferret took his paw off the bat's wing. 'Well, seeing as you're not a mouse,' he said, 'seeing as you're a bird, I'd better let you go ...'

To have one's lie believed it must be patched with truths.

149.

Hermes and the Traveller

The traveller stepped out of his house. It was early. There was a thrush singing in a tree. The traveller stopped and looked up. The sky was pearly white and empty and clean.

'Dear Hermes,' said the traveller, 'hear me, I beg, though I am a poor speaker. I am about to embark on a journey. It will be long, arduous and possibly dangerous. If you protect me, dear god, and ensure I arrive safely at my destination, I promise I will give you half of whatever I find along the way. Half, I solemnly swear, will be consecrated to you.'

The traveller set off. After some hours he saw, lying in the middle of the road, a carrying-pouch, a leather satchel, open at the top, with a long strap.

'What have we here?' said the traveller. The answer, he hoped, would be money, lots of it.

He picked up the bag and looked inside.

'Oh.'

The bag was filled with loose almonds in their shells and brown wrinkled dates.

The traveller was hungry, so he sat down at the side of the road and scoffed the lot. When he was done, rather than throwing the almond shells and the date stones into the ditch, the traveller, for he was an exceedingly cunning fellow, gathered them all up and put them back in the bag. Then he got on his feet and went on. Halfway through the afternoon, as he had expected, an altar dedicated to Hermes appeared at the side of the road.

The traveller tipped the shells and stones onto the altar top.

'So there you are, dear Hermes,' said the traveller. 'See, I am a man who always keeps his word, for here's half of what I found, the outside of the almonds and the inside of the dates.'

Consecration completed, the traveller padded on. He felt extremely pleased with himself.

Words cannot change the truth.

150.

The Swallow and the Crow

The big crow and the small swallow sat beside one another in a tree.

'Do you know who I was before I became what you see today?' said the swallow.

'I don't,' said the crow, 'but I know you're going to tell me.'

'A princess,' she said. 'I was the daughter of the king of Athens.'

'So why aren't you in your palace? Why are you here?'

'Tereus raped me, cut my tongue out so I wouldn't tell, and then I was metamorphosed into a bird.'

'It's amazing how well you tell your story,' said the crow, 'and if you actually had a tongue there'd be no holding you back, would there?'

Sitting on his throne in the great hall Zeus heard this exchange. 'Why doesn't the crow believe her?' he thought. 'She's telling the truth. Well, I'll teach that crow a lesson that'll soften his cough. Hermes!'

The lesser god bounded up.

'Put the word out,' said Zeus. 'From this day forward, crows are vermin and people should treat them as such.'

You are the master of the unspoken word, the spoken word is the master of you.

The Swallow and the Crow

9

BITTER WORDS, REBUKES, BARBS AND SAVAGERIES

151.

The Fisherman Who Was a Flute-Player

The fisherman was a marvellous flautist. One day he sat down on a rock that stuck out over the sea. He could see fish in the water below, marvellous silvery creatures moving hither and thither constantly. He took his flute out from under his cloak.

'My music is so sweet,' he said, 'those fish will jump straight out of the water and onto my lap. I know it.'

He began to play but it soon became obvious the fish weren't listening; far from jumping out and plopping into his lap, as he had imagined they would, they just stayed where they were and went on swimming around in the way fish do, speeding through the water here and there as they went about their mysterious business. He put his flute away, cast his net and pulled it in. A good haul. He emptied his catch onto the rock. The dying fish, gasping for air, jumped, writhed and wriggled.

'You impossible creatures,' he said. 'I play the flute, you won't dance. But the moment I stop, off you go … You can't stop yourselves cavorting.'

I want doesn't get.

152.

The Shipwrecked Man

The boat capsized during the storm and all who were aboard were pitched into the sea, among them a rich Athenian merchant.

As he bobbed about in the foaming waters he called,

'Athena, dear goddess, save us.' He was an Athenian and Athena was his city's patroness.

'By all means ask for her help,' shouted one of the merchant's companions, floundering in the water nearby, 'but while you're at it, don't forget to move your arms.'

By all means pray but help yourself too.

153.

The Man Unable to See

He had been blind since birth and was famous for his ability to identify animals by touch. One day a hunter brought a tiny wolf-cub, which he put into the blind man's hands.

'Perhaps it's a wolf,' said the blind man as he felt the bundle of fur, 'or perhaps it's a fox. I can't say for sure. But I do know this. I wouldn't let it anywhere near a flock of sheep.'

The label is bigger than the package.

154.

The Lion and the Man Travelling Together

A man and a lion travelling together began arguing as to who was the stronger.

At a crossroads on their route there was a statue of a man strangling a lion.

'I think that settles it,' said the man waving at the piece. 'There it is in marble. Men are stronger than you lions.'

'You're entitled to your opinion, of course,' said the lion, 'but try to use your imagination. Just think if we lions could make statues? All you'd see would be lions holding men down with *their* paws.'

One man's speech is really only half a speech.

155.

The Satyr and the Man

Though they were very different, the satyr and the man became friends …

It was winter, very cold. The satyr blew on his hands.

'Why do you do that?' asked the man, who had never seen anything like it.

The Satyr and the Man

'To warm my hands,' said the satyr.

Later that same day, in an inn, both were served soup. The satyr picked up his bowl and began to blow on it.

'Why do you do that?' asked the man. Again, he had never seen anything like it.

'To cool it,' said the satyr.

'I can't be friends with someone who blows hot and cold from the same mouth,' said the man.

He stood up and left.

'A man may learn and learn and yet remain a fool,' thought the satyr as he blew once again on his soup.

Distrusting the unknown is the easiest road.

156.

The Fox and the Bear

The bear was extolling his virtues to the fox.

'You know I won't touch anything dead,' said the bear. 'A man drops dead in the woods, I don't touch his corpse. People really respect that and they really like us for it, too.'

The fox was irritated by the bear's boasting.

'You know what would really make people like you?' he said.

'What?'

'If you only mangled their dead and left the living entirely alone.'

The sting of the reproach is the truth of it.

157.

The Axle and the Oxen

As the oxen dragged the laden cart along, the axles groaned. The noise was dreadful and it annoyed the animals.

'Hey,' one of the oxen called back. 'As usual, you complain most who suffer least. We're doing the work but you're making all the noise. Typical …'

With one's own stick one often gets the soundest beating.

158.

The Bat and the Linnet

A warm, still, dark night. The linnet sang sweetly in his cage that hung outside his captor's house.

A bat, high in the air, zipping here, zipping there, heard the linnet. He'd heard him before. 'Why does he only sing at night and never in the day?' he wondered. He decided to find out.

The bat dropped down, clung to a bar of the cage and asked, 'Why do you only sing at night?'

'Oh, that's easy,' said the linnet. 'I sang in daylight, I was heard in daylight, I was captured in daylight. So now I'm wiser, I only sing at night.'

'But you should have sung only at night when you were wild,' said the bat. 'It's too late for this now.'

'Well,' said the linnet, 'what other way do you suggest I make peace with myself for the mistake I made if not like this?'

The bat had often noticed how precautions followed rather than preceded disasters, but he had never understood just why till now. It made one feel better about one's stupidity. 'I'm so glad we had this talk,' he said, and he swept away into the night.

The future belongs to the past.

159.

The Doctor and the Old Woman

The old woman's eyesight was failing. She summoned the doctor to her house.

'Here are my terms,' she said. 'I get my sight back, I pay; I don't get my sight back, I don't pay.'

'Agreed.'

The doctor examined her eyes, applied a salve and, on his way out of her house, he took a piece of the woman's furniture. All his subsequent visits followed the same pattern: first the salve, then the larceny.

When the house was finally empty the doctor demanded his fee.

'What about our agreement?' said the old woman. 'I get my sight back, I pay; I don't get my sight back, I don't pay. You haven't done what you said, so no fee.'

The doctor had the old woman brought before the court.

'Why won't you settle his bill?' asked the judge.

'I promised to pay if he restored my sight,' the old woman said, 'but following his treatment I'm not just no better, I'm actually worse.'

'And how do you work that out?' asked the judge.

'Well, once I could see all the furniture in my house,' she said, 'but now I can't see any of it at all.'

The judge was so taken with the old woman's wit he not only exempted her from the fee but he made the doctor pay for her house to be refurnished.

None are as clever as they think.

160.

The Wood-Cutter and the Cowardly Hunter

The hunter, scouring the forest floor for the footprints of a lion, came on a wood-cutter chopping down a tree.

'There's a lion about,' said the hunter. 'Have you seen its tracks?'

'I can do better than that,' said the wood-cutter. 'I can bring you right to his lair.'

'I'm not looking for the actual lion himself,' said the hunter. 'Just the trail.'

Who stops halfway has committed no deed.

161.

The Sheep and the Young Pig

The young pig sauntered along the track. He came to a field where sheep were grazing. He stopped to look in at them.

'They look happy and contented,' he said.

He wriggled through the hedge and found himself by an old ewe.

'I know I'm a pig,' he said, 'but do you mind if I join your flock?'

'Of course not,' said the ewe.

A few days later the shepherd grabbed the pig and began hauling him towards the gate. The pig squealed and writhed.

'Stop with the roaring,' said the ewe who'd been so friendly the first day. 'We all get the same treatment but we don't make a fuss and nor should you.'

'What are you saying?' said the pig. 'When he grabs you, it's your wool or your milk he wants. In my case it's my flesh he wants, for bacon.'

If you jump up, you will also fall down.

The Sheep and the Young Pig

162.

The Bald Man and Diogenes

The philosopher met a bald man in the street.

'What have you ever done,' said the bald man, 'but say nasty things about anyone and everyone. You disgust me.'

'Which presumably,' said the philosopher, 'was what your hair said about you before it quit your ugly skull.'

He who speaks well has a shield against every blow.

163.

The Pine and the Wood-Cutters

The wood-cutter felled the pine, fashioned wedges from one of its branches and began to drive these into the trunk.

'I hate the axe that cut me down,' said the tree as it began to splinter apart, 'but I hate these wedges made of me that will tear me apart even more.'

Don't talk of ropes to the family of the man who was hanged.

164.

The Fox and the Adder

The river was in spate and an uprooted bush with an adder wrapped round a branch was being rushed along by the waters.

Standing on the bank, watching the scene, was the fox. He saw the snake.

'Hey,' he shouted to the serpent, 'don't they say the worth of a vessel is its master?'

The bush passed before the adder could reply and vanished from sight round a bend.

'Wasn't I clever to come up with that quip?' said the fox, and for the rest of the day he repeated it to every creature he met.

Sorrow and joy are next-door neighbours: this one suffers; that one rejoices.

165.

The Flute-Playing Wolf and the Dancing Kid

The wolf closed in on the herd of goats. A kid who'd lagged and who knew he was done for, turned and faced the wolf.

'I know I'm finished,' said the kid, 'but before you devour me, will you play your flute for me and let me dance?'

Seeing as he had his prey in his power, the wolf said, 'Why not?'

He played his flute and the kid danced. A pack of huntsmen's hounds, who had already heard the commotion made earlier by the herd of goats running away, now heard the flute. They came to investigate and surrounded the wolf and his prey.

The wolf, knowing he was about to be harried and killed by the dogs, turned to the kid. 'I've only myself to blame,' he said. 'The butcher should never think he's really an artist, should he? It's always going to end in tears.'

In darkness all things are black.

166.

The Castrate and the Priest

He was castrated as a child so he could sing high notes. Then he grew up and discovered, though he could still sing the high notes, that no one wanted to employ him: they wanted little boys for the high notes not fat grown men with no beards. He decided he must marry and have children. He found a woman who would have him. They married. When they went to bed he could enter her but that was all; nothing else. He sent the priest a message: 'I want to be a father. Make a sacrifice to make me one.'

The priest cut a cockerel's throat and, as its blood poured into a bowl, he prayed: 'Let him who ordered this become a father.'

Following the ceremony, the castrate called in to the temple to pay the priest.

'When I made the sacrifice,' the priest said to his visitor, 'I prayed for you to become a father. But now I meet you in person, I see there's nothing I can do; some things just can't be fixed.'

The castrate turned to go.

'Excuse me,' said the priest. 'What are you doing? You still have to pay.'

What is born a drum is beaten till death.

167.

The Camel Who Shat in the River

The camel went very carefully down the sloping river bank on his thin, spindly legs. Camels got enough mockery as it was on account of their absurd hump and their stupid mouths and their tiny ears and he had no intention of giving the knockers another reason to mock by taking a tumble now.

The camel got to the bottom of the slope safely. 'It was a mercy I didn't stumble, or worse,' he said.

The river made a gurgling, gulping watery roar.

'The river agrees,' said the camel.

He heard twittering overhead and looked up. It was the swallow, circling and watching him.

The Camel Who Shat in the River

'See anything amusing, you little gossip?' called the camel.

More twittering.

'But I didn't fall, did I? Ha, ha. You must be so disappointed.'

The camel began to wade across the river. He was halfway over and the water was up to his belly when he felt the tell-tale contractions behind. He stopped. His tail went up involuntarily. He registered his rectum's familiar opening, squeezing and expelling sensation and then his dung was out and into the river and a moment later there they were in front of him – his droppings, huge, tight, black-brown and slightly oily.

'Oh no,' he said.

His droppings were moving off now, borne away by the current.

'Typical,' said the camel, the words escaping before he could stop them. 'Some things just don't know their place, do they? They should stay behind yet they will insist on going in front.'

Again, twittering overhead. The swallow … oh no …

'Ha, ha,' she said. '"Some things just don't know their place, do they?" I heard you. This will make everyone laugh.'

She rose upwards, and the last thing she saw before flying away was the camel standing in the middle of the river, stock still, not going forward, not going back …

Indignity always finds the one who minds most.

168.

The Dog Who Did Not Get Dinner

'I shall invite my best friend to dinner tonight,' the man said.

The man's dog heard this.

'If we're having this man as a guest,' said the dog, 'then

we're jolly well having his dog too, for that animal is a very special friend of mine.'

The host's dog went to the guest's dog.

'Friend,' he said, 'your master is coming to dine with us later, and I say, you come too.'

Naturally, the other dog agreed and then he went out and told every dog in the neighbourhood, 'I'm going to a feast tonight.'

Evening came and the guest entered his host's house, his dog following. The two men, host and guest, went to the bathhouse to wash, while their two dogs, host and guest, went into the dining room to look at the food. The room was lit with oil lights. A fire burnt in the grate. A long table stood against a wall. It was covered with roasted meats, sliced and ready to eat, dishes of smooth, glistening olives, loaves of fresh, warm bread and jugs of dark red wine.

'That is some spread,' said the guest dog, wagging his tail and letting out a series of ecstatic yelps and high-pitched barks. 'I'm going to eat till I'm full,' he continued, 'and then I'm going to eat some more just to be sure I'm stuffed.'

In the nearby kitchen, the cook had heard the yelping and barking.

'That didn't sound like the master's dog,' he said. 'That sounded like a different dog. I'd better check.'

The cook hurried to the dining room and saw the guest dog.

'Hey, you,' he said, 'I don't believe you were invited.'

In one swift, fluent movement, the cook picked up the guest dog by his back legs and hurled him through the open window. The dog landed heavily on his back on the bumpy cobbles in the street outside. Then he rolled over, got to his feet and hobbled away.

'I was about to enjoy the most wonderful feast I've ever had in my life,' he said, 'when I was hurled into the street. It isn't fair …'

He passed a group of dogs to whom he'd boasted earlier about the feast he was going to have.

'You're back early,' one said. 'How was your dinner?'

'You know, I'd so much to drink,' said the dog. 'I can't even remember how I got out of the house.'

'No, of course you can't.'

The other dogs shook their heads and added, 'Can you believe it? So drunk he can't remember leaving the feast!'

The guest dog knew no dog believed him. He dropped his head and padded on.

There is no sword against derision.

169.

The Sleeping Dog and the Wolf

A spring day. The sun had warmed the stones in front of the farmyard gate and the dog lay down there and stretched out. It was glorious feeling the heat coming from both above and below.

A passing wolf saw the dog lying there. He crept up and pounced on him.

'You idiot,' said the wolf. 'If you'd been more alert and more careful you wouldn't be about to be eaten.'

'Now just hold on,' said the dog, 'and listen. Look at me. At the moment I'm pretty pitiful and thin and I won't make much of a meal. But wait, just till next week, and you'll enjoy quite a different and, if I may say, a much better dinner.

'My master's daughter is to be married this weekend. There'll be a gigantic feast here and obviously, for someone wily like me, that means all sorts of rich and fattening scraps. I'll plump up, I can promise you, and then next week, when you come back, there'll be much more of me to gorge on. What do you say?'

The wolf savoured in his mind the better and more filling meal he would enjoy when the dog was fatter. 'All right,' he said eventually, 'I'll eat you after the wedding. Good plan. I'll see you then.'

The wolf released the dog and went away ...

The wolf returned a week later. It was another boiling day. He spotted the dog lying on the roof of the stable.

'Dog,' the wolf shouted. 'Was the wedding a pleasure?'

'It was better than that. It was actually heaven,' said the dog. 'I've never eaten so much in my whole life.'

'Well, down you come,' said the wolf. 'I'm ready.'

'I don't think so,' said the dog.

'Oh, I very much do think so,' said the wolf. 'We had an agreement. It's time to be eaten.'

'Wolf,' said the dog, 'let me give you some advice. Should you ever find me lying in front of the gate down there, don't agree to wait: just gobble me up there and then.'

Greed is a bad counsellor.

170.

The Crane and the Peacock

'Well, look at you,' said the peacock to the crane. 'Your wings are – what? Blue, is it? No. They're not blue, they're grey, really, aren't they? Boring old grey. Mine, on the other hand, are a deep purple hue, the hue of a deep sea or a summer's sky at evening time, and additionally they are flecked with gold and yellow.'

'That's as may be,' said the crane, 'but with mine I mount the heights of heaven, and once I am close to the stars I sing to the great god, whereas you, like the cockerels of every farmyard, you can only mount your peahens down below. That's the only mounting you do'

It's the wearer not the garment, fool.

10

LAST GRIEFS OR
A SERIES OF EPILOGUES

171.

The Eagle and the Arrow

The eagle sat on a high rock watching for prey, convinced he was safe from danger, convinced he could not be seen.

But he was seen by a huntsman, who drew his bow, aimed and fired. His arrow curved noiselessly through the air, then buried its ugly barbed head deep in the eagle's chest. The eagle fell back and, lying on his back, his life force ebbing away, he saw that the shaft of the arrow that had felled him was fletched with feathers from his own breed.

'First, like an idiot, I expose myself,' the eagle murmured, 'and now there's this little detail of the feathers, which makes my suffering even worse.'

The well of self-blame never runs dry.

172.

The Halcyon

To keep itself safe, the mysterious halcyon bird lived exclusively at sea. Halcyons only made landfall, and this was just the females of course, in order to hatch their young. Invariably, their nesting sites were close to the water and inaccessible to people whom they did not trust.

A female made her nest on a rock at the end of a promontory that projected over the ocean. Her eggs came. She sat on them for weeks. Eventually, her chicks hatched.

One day, she went off to find them food. While she was away a storm blew up. The sea boiled and fumed. Great dark waves with white crests rose and smashed against the promontory. The halcyon's nest filled with water and the halcyon's brood, neither able to swim nor to fly, were all drowned.

Then the sea quietened. This was a short-lived squall. The halcyon returned carrying a rat in her beak. As she skimmed along the coast towards the promontory she saw the rocks below were not dry and grey as they had been when she'd set off but slick with wet and black.

'What happened?' the halcyon asked. 'Why is everything soaked?' Something was not right. Her nest came into view. Her chicks seemed to be floating. She released the rat and dropped down. Her nest was filled with water and in the water floated her little ones, bodies floppy, heads dangling, downy feathers dark with seawater, all drowned, all dead.

The halcyon landed, looked first at her chicks and then out to sea. The ocean was black with flecks of white. In the far distance it shaded to blue, and where it met the sky it was silver.

'I always thought the land was the place of danger because that's where people lived,' she said. 'So I always kept as far from it as possible and as close to sea, who I thought was my friend, as I could. But now look what has happened? It's not the land of which I was always suspicious and frightened that has hurt me but the one I trusted.'

Everyone takes his flogging in his own way.

173.

The Wolf and the Ploughman

The ploughman unharnessed his ox from the plough and led him off to the trough to drink.

While he was away a famished wolf crept up. He began to lick the oxen's sweat from inside the harness. He was so focused on the salty residue that he got his head snagged in the collar. Then, when he realised he was trapped, he frantically began to push and pull, hoping to escape. It didn't work – he was caught fast; but so hard did he struggle to get free that he actually inched the plough forwards, turning a little soil in the process.

The ploughman returned as this was happening. 'Incredible,' he said, 'a wolf driving a plough.'

The ploughman found a round, heavy stone. 'If only you would give up pillage and robbery,' he said, 'and turn to work instead.'

He smashed the stone on the wolf's head. Blood and brains everywhere. The ploughman had to haul the harness to the trough and wash it clean.

Who mixes himself with the bran will be eaten by the pigs.

174.

The Snake and the Labourer

One sunny morning, the labourer's son spotted something long and wavy lying in the long grass.

'What's that?' he said.

As he went to pick it up, the thread came to life, for it was a snake, and bit him on the hand.

'I'm bitten' the boy screamed. He collapsed and the snake wriggled off towards the hole where it hid from people.

The boy's father heard his son's cry and found him a minute later, still warm but dead. For a moment he didn't understand and then he spotted the holes in his child's hand and he knew at once who the killer was: it was the yellow adder who lived in the hole behind his house.

'I shall get that snake and chop it into pieces,' he shouted through his tears.

The labourer left his son's body and fetched his axe, then he ran to the snake's hole to kill it. There was no sign of the snake. The labourer sat down to wait. Time passed. The snake inside the hole grew thirsty and, needing to go to the river to drink and not knowing the labourer was there, he poked his head out. The labourer hurled his axe at him. He missed the snake but he hit a large stone near the hole and split it in two.

'Oh no,' the labourer thought. 'Now that he knows I'm after him, the snake's going to come and kill me first. I have to do something to stop him.'

'Come out,' he shouted. 'Let's talk. We need to be friends.'

'What?' said the snake. 'Impossible. I only have to look at the rock you've just split to know friendship's absolutely impossible, just as you'll only have to look at your son's grave after you bury him to know friendship's absolutely impossible. We're enemies and there's nothing we can do about it. Get over it.'

The crow does not roost with the phoenix.

175.

The Champion Hen and the Widow

Every day the widow's hen laid a lovely glistening egg with a smooth dark-brown shell, round at one end, slightly tapered at the other and perfect in every way.

'If I fed her more,' the widow mused, 'then surely my hen would lay twice a day.'

She doubled the bird's meal and her hen grew plump, then fat and finally gross, and then she stopped laying altogether.

Ignorance is the night of the mind, a night without moon or stars.

The Champion Hen and the Widow

176.

The Half-Blind Hind

The hind had one seeing and one blind eye. She went down to the seashore to feed and as she moved along, as she had always done, she kept her good eye facing inland, where any hunters would come from, and her bad eye on the sea. In all her years foraging down there no predators had ever menaced her from that direction.

Unfortunately, on this day, a boat passed and the men on board loosed a fusillade of arrows at her, one of which hit her and wounded her mortally. She fell to the ground.

'I kept my eye on the land believing I'd no need to watch the sea,' she said. 'Now it turns out I should have done it the other way round.'

Fate carries some on her wings and drags others to the ground.

177.

The First People and Zeus

Zeus summoned Hermes.

'The people on earth,' he said, 'I want you to pour intelligence over each one. But mind each gets exactly the same amount. We can't be having some brighter than others.'

Hermes went to earth and set to work. He was scrupulous: he poured an identical quantity of intelligence over every human.

Unfortunately, Zeus had forgotten people weren't uniform: they varied. So smaller persons got entirely covered by their allocation and were left entirely sensible; while taller people, who were not covered all over, were left stupid and even dim.

All people are the children of error.

178.

The Snake and the Bird-Catcher

The bird-catcher was in the wood looking for birds to trap. In his bag of tricks were birdlime – a nasty, sticky unguent made of pulverised mistletoe berries that held a bird's feet fast once they had touched the glue – a lure into which he could blow to imitate the calls of birds, grains of wheat and a net.

After walking for a while the bird-catcher saw a thrush. He had a lovely swelling spotted chest.

'I'll have you,' said the bird-catcher.

He stealthily approached a tree close to where the thrush sat. Quietly and slowly, he smeared some branches with bird-lime and then scattered wheat grains so they stuck to the sticky stuff. Then he found his lure and began to blow into it, watching his prey, the thrush, who was still sitting where he first saw him.

The thrush, hearing the lure, stopped singing and cocked his head in the bird-catcher's direction.

'Come on, my beauty,' the bird-catcher murmured, 'come to me.'

He put his lure away and spread his nets.

The thrush launched himself into the air and headed in the bird-catcher's direction.

The bird-catcher watched the thrush come sailing towards him through the air and then gently, oh so gently, alight on a sticky section of branch.

'Yes,' the bird-catcher murmured. 'I have you now …'

The thrush pincered a grain with his beak and found, to his surprise, it wouldn't come away. He tried then to change position, to lift first one and then the other foot, and he found he could not. Both his feet were stuck hard.

The bird-catcher opened the net wider. Just one quick cast and he would have the thrush. But before he could throw the net he felt something hard and sharp on his shin. He cried out. He had an idea he knew what it was even before he looked. And then he looked. A small brown snake was down there on the ground, coiling away from his sandaled foot. He dropped the net. He could feel the poison coursing up his leg. He sat down heavily on the ground. It hurt to breathe. A kerfuffle above. The thrush was struggling but failing to pull itself free of the birdlime that held him fast. The bird-catcher's vision was starting to blur …

'It is only impossible till it happens,' said the bird-catcher. 'I was so intent I'd have you, little thrush, so intent on my prey, I failed to see I was the prey too, didn't I? What an idiot …'

He keeled sideways and closed his eyes. He died a few moments later. The thrush, who could not escape the sticky stuff that held him fast to the branch, took a whole day to die.

It is easy to avoid a naked spear, but not a hidden sword.

179.

The Famished Dogs

The dogs hadn't eaten for days. Their skin was loose, their bones were showing and their eyes were bright and glassy. They were close to death.

'Why don't we go to the river?' one of the hungry dogs whispered to the others. The whispering was calculated to use the least energy. 'We might find something floating in the river we can eat.'

The dogs set off. They went slowly and feebly; their joints ached terribly; every step they took was agony; on top of the pain they were exhausted; all they wanted was to lie down and go to sleep. Forever …

Pain and fatigue are a fiendish combination, but the hungry dogs were desperate. They dragged themselves forward, urging each other on. 'We must get to the river … we will find something there, we're bound too …' they muttered together, over and over again.

They reached the river's edge. In the water they saw several hides, fixed with ropes to pegs driven into the bank; these hides had been left in the river by a tanner to soften.

'We can't haul the hides out – we haven't the strength,' said the dog whose idea it had been to come to the river. 'So I say we empty the river and then we can get down on to the dry riverbed and eat these skins.'

The dogs, delirious and exhausted, flopped down, dropped their heads to the water and began to lap.

'We drink, we drink,' each thought, 'and once the river's dry we'll devour those hides …'

When the tanner came the following day to check on his hides, he found, scattered along the river's bank, half a dozen emaciated dogs lying in puddles of water, their ribs showing and their distended, bloated stomachs split.

'What on earth were they up to,' asked the tanner, 'drinking and drinking till they ripped themselves open?'

The tanner was unable to answer his question, never having gone hungry.

Hunger is an infidel.

180.

The Lion and the Gnat

The sun hung high in the sky. It was a still, hot afternoon. In the shade of a eucalyptus tree a small gnat was floating around near a lion who lay stretched out on the ground. The lion was awake but resting. The gnat knew the lion, at least by reputation, and he detested this animal. In the gnat's judgement the lion was a vain, arrogant, vulgar blowhard.

'I've always wanted to take that pig down a peg or two,' thought the gnat, 'and now, seeing him lying on the ground, I

realise the gods have gifted me my chance.'

The gnat buzzed down.

'There's something I've always meant to tell you,' said the gnat.

'Which is what?' said the lion. 'That you wish you were me, king of the beasts, lord of all creation?'

'No,' said the gnat. 'What I've always wanted to tell you is this: you scratch, you rip, you bite, but anyone can. A child can do that to its mother. You're a nothing and I can prove it. So come on, we'll go head to head, and by the time we're through, you'll be begging for mercy ...'

Without waiting for the lion to reply the gnat shot up his nose. The space inside was dark and the tissue was soft and wet. The gnat began to bite vindictively, indefatigably. The lion bellowed. He lifted a paw and scratched, savagely. The skin tore. Blood welled instantly. He scratched again. More blood. But still, inside his nose, the excruciating pain continued. Desperate times call for desperate measures. Hoping to dislodge his tormentor, the lion ground his nose in the earth, mixing his blood with the dust and tearing his skin yet more in the process. But this did no good. The biting didn't stop.

The lion lifted his head to breathe and the gnat, judging his work done, zoomed out and away. From above he now looked down. He saw the lion's nose, a red, weeping, dusty mess ...

'Gnat v. Lion,' the gnat shouted, 'and the gnat triumphs, leaving his opponent, we'd all have to agree, with a bloody nose. Gnat v. Lion, one-nil, one-nil ...'

He buzzed away, ecstatic and triumphant, and ran straight into a heavy web strung among the eucalyptus's foliage.

'You fool,' said the gnat.

From the edge of the web a large black spider was advancing on him.

'So I defeated the king of the beasts,' said the gnat, 'and now a spider is about to finish me off – a spider! Some champion I've turned out to be.'

Death is the master of the world.

181.

The Stag, the Fox and the Lion

The lion was lying in his cave. He was sick. The fox put his nose into the cave's mouth. The fox and the lion were associates and from time to time the fox, as the inferior partner in the relationship, would help the lion out.

'Come in,' called the lion.

The fox entered the den.

'I'm not well and my powers have leeched away but they can be restored if you will help.'

'You can count on me,' said the fox. 'Go on.'

'The big stag who lives in the wood …'

'Yes.'

'Go to him. Tell him whatever is necessary to get him back here and, once he's inside my home, I'll get my paws into him. Only his entrails and his brain will make me well again, and so I long for them and I look to you, old friend, to help me to get them.'

'Consider it done,' said the fox.

He padded away and went deep into the wood. He found the stag standing under a tree.

'What a piece of good luck,' said the fox. 'You're exactly whom I'm looking for.'

'How's that?' said the stag. He neither liked nor trusted the fox.

'Let's start with the good news, shall we?' said the fox. 'The lion's ailing, as you know, or perhaps you don't, and he's been pondering who'll rule when he's gone. There are a number of candidates, as you'd imagine – the boar, the bear, the panther, the tiger and, last but not least, there's you, sir.

'Now, the lion's thinking is as follows: the boar is too stupid to rule – he'll mess everything up; the bear is too socially awkward and inept – he just doesn't know how to talk to anyone; the panther is too irritable and too easily provoked – he'll start a war; and the tiger, frankly, is too full of himself – on which account every animal finds him insufferable; which leaves, as doubtless you'll have noticed, just one candidate remaining – you. And, having given the matter considerable thought, His Majesty has determined, because you are the most dignified, because you are the tallest and the longest lived of all the animals, and because your antlers make you better able to kill snakes than any other creature, including lions, His Majesty has determined that you will be our next monarch.

'And now I've brought you this tremendous life-changing news, what have you to say? Go on, hurry up, I haven't got all day, you know, to stand about waiting. His Majesty is dying, he needs me by his side giving him comfort and counsel during his last hours on earth and I must hurry back to him.'

'What would you advise me to do?' said the stag, who felt overwhelmed and excited in equal measure knowing he had been selected to be the next king.

'I'd advise you to come back with me and wait in the lion's lair for His Majesty's death.'

'In the circumstances,' said the stag, 'that must be the best thing to do. I need to be there, on hand, ready to take power when His Majesty goes, don't I?'

'Yes, absolutely.'

The fox and the stag returned to the lion's cave.

'We'll creep in quietly,' said the fox. 'Don't make any noise. Go you in first.'

The stag entered. The lion, who was hiding just inside, sprang and caught the stag's ear with his paw. The stag feinted sideways, bolted out and disappeared back into the wood.

'This is some mess,' said the fox, who had seen everything.

'It's not just a mess,' said the lion, 'it's a disaster. I have to eat that creature's entrails and brain if I'm to live and he's just slipped through my grasp.'

'So what do we do now?' said the fox.

'"We" don't do anything,' said the lion. 'But "you" go back to the stag and get him to come back here and next time, I assure you, I won't fail.'

'As you wish,' said the fox. 'I'll do what I can. I can't promise more than that, can I?'

The fox went back out into the wood and began to search for the stag. He met a party of shepherds.

'Have you seen a stag?' he asked.

'With his ear bleeding?' said a shepherd.

'That's the one.'

The shepherd raised his crook and pointed the way. The fox ran on, sniffing the ground, scenting the stag's blood, and eventually he found the stag standing by a large mossy rock, with his ear bleeding and his dun pelt spattered with blood.

'Stay away,' the stag shouted. 'One step closer and I will gore you with my antlers, an experience, I promise, you'll not enjoy.'

The fox stopped. 'What's with this anger?' said the fox, 'I don't understand.'

'You lured me into the cave and, once I was inside, your friend the lion went for me. I was nearly done for and would have been, only I got away.'

'What do you mean you were nearly done for?' said the fox. 'You idiot, you weren't nearly done for. His Majesty just wanted your ear, only not literally – don't you get it? He wanted to talk to you; he wanted to tell you everything you will need to know when you become king. Everything! He was a bit abrupt, I grant you that, but our monarch is dying. He doesn't have time to do things in the old way, observing the usual courtesies and protocols. He could go at any moment. And there is so much you need to be told, so much. So stop with the whingeing and the complaining just because you got a little scratch and follow me back to His Majesty. And, by the way, in case you think otherwise, we haven't got time to dilly-dally. His Majesty is so angry that you wouldn't listen to what he had to say but took fright and ran off, he's thinking of nominating the wolf to rule after his death. The wolf! Can you believe that? He wasn't even on the shortlist. He's totally and completely unscrupulous. If he's put in charge, we animals are finished, obviously. So, come on, come with me, come back to the cave and listen to your king, hear what he has to tell you, and then when he dies, which will be soon, you will take charge, you will become king.'

'I don't know,' said the stag. Half of him wanted to go back to the cave with the fox, for he couldn't imagine a greater honour than being king, and the knowledge of all the adulation that would flow to him once he was on the throne was thrilling, but the other half of him didn't want to go. The lion had tried to kill him and would do it again, he was sure. The fox, an excellent judge of every situation, sensed the other's equivocal position.

'Listen,' said the fox. 'I understand why you wouldn't want to come back. Really, I do. How do you know what is true? How do you know who to trust? Well, hear me out: I swear by the leaves on the trees and the springs that dot this wood and by everything else you can see or hear around us, you have no reason to fear the lion. None. He will not harm you. As for me, my interest is in the future. I have always served His Majesty the lion, but soon His Majesty will be dead and then you will be the new king, and it is my wish that I also serve you when that time comes. That's why I'm here, now. It's a signal of my intention to serve you.'

The stag was persuaded. He returned to the cave. The lion was waiting and ready. As soon as the stag came in he pounced. He caught the stag and toppled him. The stag tried to stand but before he could get to his feet the lion mauled his throat, slicing open the artery that ran from the stag's heart to his head. The stag juddered. His blood pumped and gushed and it wasn't very long before the stupid animal was dead.

The lion, who was famished, immediately got to work on the carcass. He split the stag in half from head to tail and ate the lungs and rest of his viscera. Then he peeled the muscle, split the bones and set about sucking the jellied marrow out of them, a long and noisy process. The fox, meantime, eyed the grey, wobbly, creased brain sitting on one side of the stag's cranium.

'I know the lion wants it,' he thought. 'Didn't he say as much at the start of this escapade. But he can't have everything. Something must come to me. I must have a reward for all I've done for the old tyrant and that brain must be my reward.'

The lion was busy digging marrow out of a thick bone and not looking. Here was his chance, the fox realised. He snatched up the brain with his little teeth and swallowed it whole in a single gulp.

The lion finished the marrow. 'Now, where's the brain?' he said, peering at the stag's split skull. 'I don't understand, I can't see it.'

The fox retreated to the cave's mouth.

'That's because there isn't one,' said the fox.

'What, no brain?' said the lion. 'Of course there's a brain. Every creature has a brain. I'm sure it was here.'

'That might be true for the rest of the animals but not for this stag. Think about it, Your Majesty. How else can we explain his stepping into your den not once but twice, and the second time after having had his ear mauled. Of course he doesn't have a brain. Surely you see that.'

The fox turned and fled, leaving the lion standing there, puzzled and unsure as he stared at the two halves of the stag's head. 'No brain?' he said. 'Surely that can't be right.'

He who has an associate has a master.

182.

The Fox, the Bear and the Lion

Ambling along together, side by side, the lion and the bear, who were friends, came across the carcass of a fawn.

'Ah,' said the lion, 'my dinner.'

'I beg to differ,' said the bear.

'I thought you bears were famous for not eating carrion,' said the lion.

'Not me,' said the bear. 'I eat anything. So stand aside. I saw the faun first. It's mine. Back off.'

'No, you back off,' said the lion. 'It's mine.'

The lion and the bear tore into each other, biting, scratching and mauling each other's bodies. They were heavy. They were well matched. Each inflicted much damage on the other. Then both collapsed from their respective and very considerable injuries and lay on the ground, bleeding, panting, unable to move.

At this moment a fox, who had been watching the whole scene from behind a tree, scurried out.

'Who's this coming?' murmured the lion.

'The fox,' said the bear. 'Heading our way!'

'What?'

'He'll have the fawn, I don't doubt.'

The bear was right. The fox darted between himself and the lion, took the fawn's body in his mouth and began to drag it away.

'You know what we are?' said the lion.

'Tell me,' said the bear.

'Fools,' said the lion. 'All this trouble tearing lumps out of one another, and for what? So that little thief can take what we found.'

'Yes,' the bear murmured, 'we're idiots, absolute idiots.'

We are fools one to another.

183.

The Lion and the Wolf Proud of His Shadow

Evening. A sun hung low in the sky and its warm, yellow, buttery light fell almost slantwise on the open ground across which the wolf was slowly walking, his eye captivated by the huge elongated shadow cast by his body that stretched ahead.

'What a shadow,' said the wolf. 'I doubt there's a shadow as mighty as mine anywhere else on earth. What am I saying? Of course there isn't. That's the greatest shadow on earth and it's cast by the greatest animal on earth, without a shadow of a doubt, ha ha.'

The wolf smirked.

'Without a shadow of a doubt,' he repeated, 'the greatest shadow on earth.'

He had a weakness for puns, no matter how weak they were.

'And as the owner of the greatest shadow on earth,' the wolf continued, 'it obviously follows I should be king of the animals.' He was on a roll now. 'Of course. Who else? The greatest animal who casts the greatest shadow, must be king. It can be no one else but me.'

The wolf strutted on, pondering his imminent elevation.

'Me! King of the animals,' he whispered. 'Yes!'

It was a lovely idea. He completely lost himself in it. So much so, he didn't notice the lion tracking him. He didn't hear the lion running towards him. He only noticed when the lion had leapt, caught him and knocked him to the ground and was about to rip his throat open.

'King of the animals,' said the wolf. 'No, that was pure presumption, and look where it's got me? I let my fancies run away with me. I should know … If a man puts a cord around his neck, God will provide someone to pull it.'

'Shut up,' said the lion and he bit down hard.

Those who walk on stilts of glass, beware: they are easily broken.

184.

The Lion, the Cock and the Ass

Under normal circumstances no lion would enter the farmyard. It was too close to the farmhouse where people lived and so far too risky. But the lion hadn't eaten for days and he was famished. So he jumped over the wall to see what he could find and what he found was the ass and the cock who were penned in the yard together. The lion rushed at the ass.

'Cock-a-doodle-doo,' crowed the cock.

The noise was terrible to hear and for the lion, who like all lions was terrified of the noise that cocks make, it was doubly terrible. He baulked and jumped back over the wall the way he had come in.

'The lion's frightened,' shouted the ass, who'd been watching everything. 'He's turned tail and run!'

Without thinking, the ass jumped the gate and charged after the lion. What did he have to fear from this lion? Nothing, he believed.

In the yard the cock was still crowing but the further the lion went, the ass in pursuit, the less audible the crowing became and therefore the less afraid the lion became. Eventually the pair were so far from the farmyard the lion couldn't hear the cock at all. He stopped, turned, saw the ass coming and, as he now no longer felt afraid, he jumped at the ass and felled him to the ground.

'Imbecile,' said the lion. 'You weren't made for war, yet for a moment there you thought you were. And now look where that's got you?'

Iron destroys and rusts itself.

185.

The Lion, the Ass and the Fox

The ass and the fox went into partnership and sallied out to forage for food together. They had only gone a little way through the countryside when they saw the lion heading their way.

'Oh no,' said the ass. 'He's going to have us for supper, for sure.'

'Not necessarily both of us,' thought the fox. He formulated a plan on the pull-the-ear-and-the-head-follows principle.

'Let's split up,' he said, 'and run in separate directions. That way the lion will get confused, not know who to run after and perhaps, who knows, if the god's smile, we'll both get away.'

The ass, always easy to encourage, always easy to direct, said, 'Good idea.'

The partners split – the ass fleeing one way and the fox the other. But once they were apart the fox, rather than running away, turned back and ran towards the lion. Once the predator was within hailing distance, the fox stopped.

'If I help you catch the ass,' he said, 'will you spare me?'

'Why would I do that,' said the lion, 'when I can have both of you?'

'I'll manage things so you won't have to make any effort at all,' said the fox. 'I'll deliver the ass wrapped in a bow, so to speak.'

'Go on then,' said the lion. 'This I want to see.'

The fox ran after the ass and caught up with him.

'Listen,' he said. 'I've laid a false trail going that way, and the lion, thinking that's where we've gone, is going that way too. So follow me now, and we'll go the other way, and we'll get far, far away from that devil.'

'Oh, right,' said the ass, gullible as always. 'Thank you. Yet again, dear friend, you've saved the day.'

The fox led, the ass followed. The path they were on, unknown to the ass, led to a hidden pit. It had been dug by hunters some months before. The fox knew exactly where it was but the ass didn't. When they reached the pit, the fox stepped sideways and avoided falling in, whereas the ass did not step sideways and so did fall in. It was a deep pit, as deep as the ass was high, and when he recovered from the fall and looked up, the ass knew he was trapped.

'Fox, help me,' he called. 'I've fallen into a hole.'

But the fox wasn't there to hear him. The fox had turned and was running back to the lion. He found him where he had left him, more or less.

'Your dinner awaits,' he said. 'The ass is in the pit, the one the hunters dug on the path a few months ago. He's waiting for you to come and devour him.'

'Is that so?' said the lion. 'Well, he can wait. There's no hurry is there?'

He swiped his paw and broke the fox's neck with a single blow, and then he dragged his sharp claws along the fox's body laying bare his delicate inner parts, his heart, his liver, his kidneys, the bits the lion relished.

The lion took his first mouthful. In the distance he heard the ass braying, desperate for his false friend the fox to return and save him.

'Yes,' said the lion, 'all in all, this has been a very good afternoon.'

He who flies high falls low.

186.

The Wolf and the Ass Who Pretended to Be Lame

The ass was grazing quietly in the small meadow at the foot of the mountain when he realised he was not alone. There was a wolf stealthily working his way towards him.

'It's too late to run,' the ass said. 'The wolf's too close. Only trickery will get me out of this fix.'

The ass began to walk up and down the meadow, and as he walked he limped theatrically. Anyone watching would have thought the ass could only walk with extreme difficulty. Certainly this was what the wolf thought.

'What's the matter with your leg?' he said when he came up.

'Oh, don't ask,' said the ass.

'Stone in your hoof?'

'No, no, a stone I could stand,' said the ass. 'No, it's a blooming great thorn, the size of a nail, a black, vicious, nasty so-and-so, and it's right smack bang in the middle of my hoof. Of course I've only myself to blame. I jumped a fence and landed on it – that's how I picked it up – and ever since then it's crippled me. That's why I couldn't run when I saw you coming. And now, seeing as you're here, I wonder would you do me a great favour before you eat me? Take the thorn out and give me a moment's relief before I go. This will also mean you won't get the thorn in your mouth later, which would be frightful, so you'll be doing yourself, as well as me, a favour.'

'All right,' said the wolf, 'seeing as you put it so nicely.'

The ass lifted the leg he'd limped on, the hind left one. The wolf bent down and peered at the ass's hoof.

'Whereabouts is it?' he said. 'I can't see it.'

'Right in the middle. Look closer.'

The wolf bent lower. The ass lashed back with his leg with all his might. He caught the wolf smack in the middle of his mouth and knocked out his four front teeth, top and bottom.

The wolf let out a blood-curdling howl. The ass bolted. Blood and teeth fragments were all over the wolf's lips and chin.

'What was I thinking?' wailed the wolf. In the distance he heard the ass thundering away, his bellowing bray clear and bright. 'I was brought up to be a butcher, plain and simple.

What on earth possessed me to try my hand at doctoring? I should know by now. Do not lose your old path for the sake of a new one.'

Habit is a suit of iron and he who takes it off hurts himself.

187.

The Son and the Painted Lion

An old and somewhat timid man had an only son who loved to hunt. One night the father dreamt his son was out in the country chasing after a lion. His son had a spear in one hand and a net in the other. His plan was to corner the lion at the end of a gully, net him and stab him to death. But the gully had a way out the son didn't know of that was different to the way in. The lion got away, doubled round, crept back in and mauled his son to death.

The father woke in darkness, sweating and weeping.

'Oh, what a dreadful dream,' he exclaimed. 'My boy is going to be killed by a lion. But I don't have to accept the future the dream foretells. No, I don't. I can refuse it. I shall build a villa, high in the mountains, where there aren't any lions for him to chase after. I shall put paintings on the walls of all the animals he's killed, lions included, to keep him company. And I'll send him there to live. Yes, that's what I'll do. Good plan, old fellow.'

He built the faraway villa and ordered his son to live there …

Time passed. The son was miserable. He hated the villa. It was lonely. It was far away from everywhere, especially the places where he had once hunted. And there was almost nothing to do. All he did every day to amuse himself was stare at the sky and watch the eagles circling, while every evening all he did was stare at the animals painted on the walls and remember the times he had hunted these animals for real.

The Son and the Painted Lion

One night the son drank heavily and then began to pad from painting to painting, staring sadly at each in turn. He came to the lion picture.

'Had my father not had the dream of the lion that he had,' he shouted at the painting, 'he wouldn't have built this prison and had you painted on the wall along with all the other animals to keep me quiet. I hate you all but I hate you most, you know.'

He punched the wooden panel the painting was on, aiming for the lion's face, intending to blind him. The panel split and a splinter lodged beneath the son's fingernail. The next morning, sober again, his head pounding with a hangover, the son tried to pull the splinter out. It broke. His finger became infected. It swelled up, followed by the hand and then the arm. Fever set in. It was sepsis. He slipped into a coma and died.

After the funeral the father had the damaged painting of the lion repaired and brought to his own villa and every day, for the rest of his life, the old man looked at the painting and had the same thought: 'That, I'm sure, was my son's favourite painting.'

Ignorance and incuriosity are two very soft pillows.

188.

The Dolphin and the Monkey

To amuse themselves on the long voyage home to Greece, many of the passengers on board had brought along either monkeys or Maltese terriers.

As the ship neared Cape Sounion, a promontory near Athens, a storm rose. It was vicious and unforgiving. Huge quantities of water shipped aboard and the boat capsized and every living thing was thrown into the furious sea, including a small black monkey with a long curly tail.

The Dolphin and the Monkey

A dolphin, cruising nearby, saw the monkey bobbing on the surface. He assumed it was a person, rose from below, hoisted the animal onto his smooth, long back and pointed himself towards land, with the intention of taking what he assumed was a person to safety …

After several hours in the water Piraeus, the port of the city of Athens, came into view.

'You're an Athenian, I presume,' said the dolphin.

'I am,' said the monkey. He knew an Athenian was a person from Athens because his master, now drowned he presumed, was such a person.

'And not just any old Athenian,' the monkey continued. 'Normally, I wouldn't like to talk about this but seeing as you've asked, and seeing as you've helped me like you have, I feel I must answer your question honestly and openly. My people, my parents, are rather important Athenians, as it happens, which in turn makes me a rather illustrious person too.'

'And do you know Piraeus?' the dolphin continued.

'Piraeus?' the monkey said. Who was this Piraeus? He'd never heard of him before. Well, he must answer and whatever he did he mustn't show his ignorance.

'Of course I know Piraeus,' said the monkey. 'He's one of my best friends. Do you know him?'

'No, I've never met him,' said the dolphin, 'nor will I, for the simple reason he doesn't exist. He's a place, not a person.'

The dolphin was disgusted with the lie the monkey had told him. He dropped downwards and the monkey suddenly found himself no longer riding along on the dolphin's back but splashing about in the water, trying to swim towards land, and not getting anywhere particularly fast.

He struggled on for several hours. He got thirsty. He got hungry. His strength waned. Hope deserted him. In the end, he drowned.

Not to speak is the flower of wisdom.

189.

The Professional Mourners and the Rich Man

The rich man had two daughters. One was bitten by a wild dog; she contracted rabies and died. A funeral was planned and, to swell numbers and to make the occasion more impressive, the father hired some professional mourners.

The day of the funeral came. The professional mourners came in perfect funeral clothes, and during the service and the subsequent interment of the body in the family's mausoleum, their sobbing, stamping and shrieking outdid the family's.

In the evening the surviving daughter and her mother were at home by the fire.

'It's all topsy-turvy,' said the daughter. 'Today, at the service, we, the family, were so much less impressive than the professionals. Those women had no connection with my sister or us, yet look how much better they were? They, not us, were the ones who looked like proper mourners.'

'Yes,' said the mother, 'that's true. But don't forget they did it for money so they're bound to make a better fist of things than we would, who weren't paid.'

Necessity will buy and sell.

190.

The Trumpeter

The battle was over. Night had fallen.

'All prisoners stand,' the guards shouted.

The battered and defeated soldiers from the losing side stood.

'And, quick march …'

The weary prisoners began to trudge. They knew exactly where they were going – a high cliff. When they got there they would wait out the night and then, as the sun rose, because dawn was when it was done, they'd be tossed onto the brutal jagged rocks at the foot of the cliff and from there their corpses, instead of being taken by their wives and mothers, tenderly washed, prepared for burial and given their last rites, would be carried out to sea and devoured by sharks.

The prisoners and their guards reached the cliff top. It was still dark.

'Right, you scum,' the guards shouted, 'sit down.'

Everyone sat except for the trumpeter.

'Permission to address the commanding officer?' he requested the nearest guard.

'Granted.'

The guard led the trumpeter to his commanding officer. The officer was standing on the edge of the cliff staring out to sea. He was waiting for the sun to show the top of his head over the horizon. As soon as this happened he would give the order to start the killings.

'Prisoner wishes to speak,' said the guard.

'Go on,' said the officer. 'Spit it out. What is it?'

'I'm not really a soldier,' the trumpeter began, 'and so I don't think I ought to be included in this business.'

'What do you mean?' said the officer. 'You're one of the enemy, aren't you? You were captured with this rabble weren't you?'

He pointed at the prisoners slumped on the ground, grubby, sullen and morose.

'So you get thrown over,' the officer continued. 'It's what we do. You lose, you go over. If we'd lost and I'd been captured, I'd be sitting on the ground waiting my turn.'

'It's true I was taken at the same time as these other prisoners,' said the trumpeter, 'but I'd no weapon when I surrendered, you know. All I had was my trumpet. I'm the trumpeter. I've never used a weapon in my life; I've never hurt anyone in my life with a weapon. I just play music, that's all.'

'You didn't kill us, or try to kill us,' said the officer, 'at least not directly. I grant you that. But you and your bloody trumpet roused these wretches to bestir themselves, gather their arms and come at us, hoping to kill us. You may never have carried a weapon like them but it's you who got the battle going and, if anything, that makes you actually more eligible for execution than any of the men behind.'

The golden rim of the sun hoisted itself ever so slightly above the horizon.

'There he is,' said the officer to the trumpeter. 'You'll go first. Enjoy the journey down.'

He hurled the trumpeter over the edge and then watched him falling, wailing terribly as he dropped away, before smashing onto the rocks at the bottom and splitting open. A great pool of red and white oozed from the trumpeter's head. Then a great wave came over the rock on which the body lay. It lifted the corpse and carried it into the sea and it took all the blood and brain that was smeared everywhere as well, and after it was gone the rocks were left clean and wet and shiny and ready for the next body.

'Let's go,' the officer shouted. 'Let's get this done.'

The guards blew their whistles and kicked all the prisoners to their feet. Some began to pray; others to weep or snivel. The first man was dragged towards the edge. Those behind him watched and waited, stunned and appalled …

A fox does not smell his own stench.

List of Illustrations

A Note on the Text

All fables are taken from Professor Émile Chambry's magisterial
Ésope Fables: Texte établi et traduit par Émile Chambry
(Collection des Universités de France, Paris, 1927), of which
the standard English language version is *Aesop: The Complete
Fables*, translated by Olivia and Robert Temple (Penguin Classics,
London, 1998). For interested readers, the key below identifies
first the Chambry number and then the number in this text.

Prologue
    Chambry 303

1: Caprice, Arrogance and the Exercise
of Arbitrary Power
    Chambry 1 = 1
    Chambry 8 = 2
    Chambry 12 = 3
    Chambry 23 = 4
    Chambry 34 = 5
    Chambry 66 = 6
    Chambry 76 = 7
    Chambry 95 = 8
    Chambry 104 = 9
    Chambry 101 = 10
    Chambry 109 = 11
    Chambry 118 = 12
    Chambry 119 = 13
    Chambry 121 = 14
    Chambry 126 = 15
    Chambry 181 = 16

Chambry 194 = 17
Chambry 221 = 18
Chambry 262 = 19
Chambry 357 = 20

2: Irreconcilability, Conflict
and Vengeance
Chambry 3 = 21
Chambry 4 = 22
Chambry 19 = 23
Chambry 21 = 24
Chambry 44 = 25
Chambry 45 = 26
Chambry 55 = 27
Chambry 103 = 28
Chambry 117 = 29
Chambry 155 = 30
Chambry 196 = 31
Chambry 209 = 32
Chambry 244 = 33
Chambry 254 = 34
Chambry 298 = 35
Chambry 299 = 36
Chambry 319 = 37
Chambry 328 = 38
Chambry 331 = 39
Chambry 336 = 40

3: Self-Deception, Stupidity
and Idiocy
Chambry 2 = 41
Chambry 5 = 42
Chambry 11 = 43
Chambry 15 = 44
Chambry 32 = 45
Chambry 39 = 46
Chambry 48 = 47

Chambry 65 = 48
Chambry 69 = 49
Chambry 77 = 50
Chambry 82 = 51
Chambry 83 = 52
Chambry 89 = 53
Chambry 102 = 54
Chambry 112 = 55
Chambry 114 = 56
Chambry 123 = 57
Chambry 185 = 58
Chambry 265 = 59
Chambry 308 = 60

4: Ambition,
Overweening and
Overreach
Chambry 10 = 61
Chambry 20 = 62
Chambry 29 = 63
Chambry 30 = 64
Chambry 33 = 65
Chambry 46 = 66
Chambry 50 = 67
Chambry 51 = 68
Chambry 58 = 69
Chambry 61 = 70
Chambry 72 = 71
Chambry 84 = 72
Chambry 98 = 73
Chambry 108 = 74
Chambry 110 = 75
Chambry 135 = 76
Chambry 224 = 77
Chambry 346 = 78
Chambry 351 = 79
Chambry 352 = 80

5: Selfishness,
Self-Interest and
Self-Love
>Chambry 26 = 81
>Chambry 27 = 82
>Chambry 37 = 83
>Chambry 41 = 84
>Chambry 47 = 85
>Chambry 52 = 86
>Chambry 56 = 87
>Chambry 74 = 88
>Chambry 85 = 89
>Chambry 86 = 90

6: Gloating and
Heartlessness
>Chambry 31 = 91
>Chambry 40 = 92
>Chambry 43 = 93
>Chambry 88 = 94
>Chambry 91 = 95
>Chambry 92 = 96
>Chambry 99 = 97
>Chambry 106 = 98
>Chambry 116 = 99
>Chambry 132 = 100
>Chambry 160 = 101
>Chambry 165 = 102
>Chambry 186 = 103
>Chambry 204 = 104
>Chambry 205 = 105
>Chambry 236 = 106
>Chambry 241 = 107
>Chambry 264 = 108
>Chambry 339 = 109
>Chambry 355 = 110

7: Jealousy, Covetousness
and Greed
>Chambry 16 = 111
>Chambry 18 = 112
>Chambry 35 = 113
>Chambry 38 = 114
>Chambry 57 = 115
>Chambry 62 = 116
>Chambry 146 = 117
>Chambry 163 = 118
>Chambry 175 = 119
>Chambry 227 = 120
>Chambry 234 = 121
>Chambry 237 = 122
>Chambry 239 = 123
>Chambry 246 = 124
>Chambry 253 = 125
>Chambry 258 = 126
>Chambry 272 = 127
>Chambry 275 = 128
>Chambry 278 = 129
>Chambry 353 = 130

8: Cunning, Guile
and Insight
>Chambry 6 = 131
>Chambry 9 = 132
>Chambry 13 = 133
>Chambry 17 = 134
>Chambry 22 = 135
>Chambry 73 = 136
>Chambry 78 = 137
>Chambry 79 = 138
>Chambry 80 = 139
>Chambry 96 = 140
>Chambry 109 = 141